THE
HEALER

A NOVEL

— • —

LLOYD MATTHEW THOMPSON

STARFIELD

THE HEALER: A NOVEL
by Lloyd Matthew Thompson
Copyright © 2014 Starfield Press - All Rights Reserved

First printing 2014
Second printing 2020

Paperback ISBN: 978-0692223772

Fiction • Fantasy • Science Fiction • Metaphysical/New Age • Spiritual

Starfield Press
www.StarfieldPress.com
Oklahoma City, OK

Cover art: *Malvine, Dying in the Arms of Fingal*
by Anne-Louis Girodet, c. 1800

Cover design by Lloyd Matthew Thompson

To those who know
even healers need healing.

THE
HEALER

A NOVEL

• PROLOGUE •

SHE HAD NEVER FOUND anything in the world like rain. It never ceased to amaze her how each drop was so entirely and utterly different.

Although there were billions of individual drops in even the smallest shower, if one went deep enough, each drop was so unique it could not even begin to be said one drop was like another. Each had been on its own journey around the world countless times. Each drop had gathered images and impressions of all the places it had been, each person it had touched, and every *other* drop it had come into contact with. Each drop remembered, in an endless chain of interconnected information that now coursed through her awareness the instant it touched her naked body.

She *felt* it.

Even after countless lifetimes, rain still managed to leave her marveling. She couldn't help but spread her arms and throw back her head, whether she was reading the rain for business or pleasure.

It was as if little pieces of the world had been laid directly at her feet.

When one opened to such an experience, it was

extremely easy to get lost inside it, even for one so accomplished and practiced. It required a total abandonment of self, a deep releasing of all but the act itself. The simultaneous blending of highness and humbleness it twisted round and round within one created a vortex that was effortlessly able to blot out all other senses or realities.

And realities were what she knew.

She had been thoroughly fascinated when scientists published the first illustrations of DNA—the deoxyribonucleic acid that is the basis of all physical life. The spiraling she had always experienced when reading the rain had been depicted perfectly in the strands of the DNA coils and helixes shown weaving intricate and marvelous patterns as distinct as each droplet of rain itself. The biographical and historical data that could be extracted from a single strand of DNA was unable to be fully comprehended by the human mind, but even that data was limited to certain family lines, and often only certain regions.

But rain—or, more specifically, water—could relate so much more information to her. If the moment was right, virtually everything everywhere could be found. There was nothing that was not connected to *something*.

She stood atop the largest mausoleum of Grace View Cemetery, arms spread, absorbing the raindrops. Long, black hair hung from her tilted head, dripping water down her back, a mirror of the water dripping from her pointed breasts in front, and from her fingertips to each side.

Closing her eyes, she smiled into the sky and the downpour. This had quickly become her favorite perch for reading rain. Discovering this graveyard and making it her own had made her relocation from southern Europe considerably easier, if she had ever had such a thing as a hard time with her moves. She had found long ago that having a secure space she could open completely in gave her an upper hand that had proved to be invaluable for her countless times. It was the first thing she sought each time she moved, whether the move was necessary, or if it was of her own free will. The places she chose as her own weren't always considered so dismal by the public eye as a graveyard was, but the secluded spot she had found in the center of this massive memorial park was the model location for the privacy required to truly focus on the energies.

With her feet firmly planted just over shoulder width apart, she allowed the chill of the rain on her light brown skin to shock her into an altered state of mind.

She slowly inhaled the cool air deep into her lungs. *Come to me,* she willed, then released the air faster than she had brought it in. As the last bit of breath left her body on the third repetition, her mind rode the tidal wave of energy it sent out, completing her shift to the other world.

Directing her awareness fully toward the drops of water pelting her bare skin, she began to perceive the images and sensations each held inside. It first came as a momentary cacophony of noise flooding her senses, then quickly began to separate and clarify as she expertly focused on specific areas. She spiraled deeper still, searching thousands of individual raindrops for what she desired.

A young man, freshly into puberty, gloomily crosses a small stream, leaving the young woman of his heart behind as he heads for the desert and his rite of passage swam into her awareness. An overweight man slips on an icy sidewalk, sending the stack of colorfully wrapped gifts in his arms sailing in all directions as he lands in a pile of snow, unable to get back up. A shot of ecstatic energy zipped by as two forbidden lovers stole an orgasmic moment in a public swimming pool. 1967.

This time, this country, she directed. The visions shifted.

A young woman screams in frustration as she tries to change a flat tire on her vehicle by herself, freezing to death and soaked to the bone from the downpour. An old man in

1923 with nothing left to lose dances in a puddle and laughs hysterically because it reminds him of the time he and his new bride did that very thing the first night of their honeymoon in the islands.

This city... There.

The energy she had felt distantly, and had traveled to this place for, was there. Rarely had such an energy been felt by her from so far, so close to the moment, in such real-time. She typically found her leads from a variety of news reports or stories spread by word of mouth, then moved as close as possible to physically investigate more easily via her gift—truly living in two worlds at once.

She always paid very close attention to all that happened around her, rain or no rain, and new breakthroughs being made in technology promised to make her efforts even easier in the future.

Now, at last, weeks of waiting for a thunderstorm were immediately forgiven as she zeroed in on the person she had felt.

She now found it was a male, currently moving in a hurry from a vehicle to a building in an awkward way, trying to avoid being thoroughly drenched. She began tracing the line of his DNA before she lost him into the building. The information the raindrops fed back to her sent a shock through her system.

Could this actually be?

She began to drop her arms and shift back into her own perceptions. She inhaled a deep breath to sever her connection with the rain, then froze.

Wait. What was that?

She quickly reentered the connection and searched the water drops for confirmation. Something was building, a pressure in the energy increasing. She waited, fully alert.

There!

The discharge of energy sent a shock wave that nearly knocked her from the crypt.

What is going on here?

She opened her eyes and shifted back to her own physical vision. Her eyes swept the cemetery before her while her mind raced.

Only one thing could explain what had just happened, and it was the one thing she had dreaded above all—had nearly convinced herself would *not* happen.

But this was it.

She was sure of it.

*We are healed of a suffering
only by experiencing it
to the full.*

—Marcel Proust

• CHAPTER 1 •

He HAD ONLY WANTED to stop her screaming. The thought of it even now sent shivers through his entire body. How a human voice was capable of making such a hideous noise, he still hadn't figured out—but he had heard it once before, in another place. It had broken him.

His body flew into action.

They had gone to the place where the people gave money. His mother had promised it would be the last stop that day, then they would be getting the sundae that had been promised him. He had worked especially hard at being very still all day as his mother talked with all the different men wearing stiff-looking clothes, sitting behind huge metal desks. He didn't understand why it was so important for his mother to talk to all these people, especially since she seemed so upset about it, but he knew she would keep her promise if he behaved. He could tell when she was telling the truth or not.

Now it was almost time. He had made it through the entire day, and was smiling brightly at the thought of getting a sweet so soon before dinner as they entered that last building. Even the rain that had begun pouring on them did not dampen his mood.

His smile faded as his mother gently tugged him along to claim a place in line. His head turned and his eyes immediately took in the man and the woman.

"Stay close to me, baby."

He moved closer to his mother, but never took his eyes off the couple. They sat occupying two chairs in a row of chairs lining the waiting room, the woman's red dress matching the red of the upholstery nearly perfectly. The man's hand rested on the woman's leg beside him. The man's face was unreadable, staring straight ahead, in line with his large and powerful body. The woman appeared to be trying to mask the fact she was in a state of extreme distress, but he clearly remembered recognizing this about her true emotional state, even at that age. Her mouth made no movement as she stole quick, sweeping glances around the room, but the horrible screaming was most definitely coming from her.

He knew.

The dozen other people nearby made no move to help. Why didn't they do anything? Couldn't they hear her screaming? He wanted to cover his ears, but could not seem to get his own body to move. He wished she would stop.

But it was more than just the scream. Something about it seemed... familiar. He didn't know the woman. He had never heard any sort of scream like that in his life before. It went on and on and on. He had only wanted to be done with the stops. His mother had promised him a sundae, and she was telling the truth. Why did they have to come in this building with the screaming woman?

Suddenly, he no longer felt four years old.

He felt as if he were looking down from a great height. Crowds and crowds of people spread out far below him, yet not so far below that it was impossible to make out what was happening.

They were moving.

They were not only moving, they were fighting.

His eyes widened as he saw people violently attacking

other people, thrashing and hitting and cutting and kicking. He was paralyzed as the red pools of blood gathered in the streets quicker than he ever imagined it could, catching flashing glares of the hot sun nearly directly overhead, only to be splashed apart by another foot trying to escape harm, another body falling to the earth.

Tears were streaming down his face—tears of utter helplessness, tears of the pain he was witnessing, tears of the knowledge that this was not enemy against enemy below him, but brother against brother, mother against daughter.

And the scream was piercing his ears.

It did not come from the masses below, but from somewhere much closer to him.

Mouth still agape, and beard still moist, he turned his head to the left and saw the source—a woman in a long white and maroon dress.

Suddenly, he was back in the money building—the banker's, he knew now. A jolt went through his four-year-old body as he realized with horror the woman in red was looking directly at him. The scream continued to split his eardrums as he watched the man finally move his head to look at the woman, then turn to follow her gaze.

The man's eyes met his with an unchanging coldness. Did the man know he could hear the woman screaming? Did the man himself even know she was screaming?

"Audi, come along."

He shuffled sideways until he felt the familiar rough scratchiness of his mother's wool overcoat, unable to break the man's gaze. He moved his hand to grip tight to her sleeve. The man seemed to be looking straight into him. Who was this man?

"Stay with me," his mother said. "We're next, then all done."

The man released him as he broke eye contact to greet another man coming up to the couple. The woman rose to her feet beside the man as he shook hands with the banker.

Smiling and nodding as the banker gestured them toward a side office, the man turned and gave Audi a final direct glare.

Abruptly, the woman began to run toward the entrance of the building, scrambling around the startled banker. The big man whipped around and lunged for the woman, catching her roughly by the arm. She immediately opened her mouth and screamed aloud, adding it to the apparently silent screaming she had never stopped doing.

Every head in the building now turned at the commotion. The banker was tripped to the floor as the woman screamed and screamed. She fought with all she had, but the man had a firm grip on her she could not shake.

Audi's body flew into action.

A distant part of him was dimly aware his mother was shouting his name. An even farther part of him was aware of the screaming in the high place over the crowds simultaneously. Still another part of him was running toward the man and woman, ahead of the others in the bank. It was all his fault, wasn't it? He did it. No—he didn't do it. It was all his fault because he didn't do it.

He saw the man's eyes widen in surprise as he turned and saw Audi just before Audi reached out and touched the man's smooth tan coat. The momentum he had gained from his run pressed his hand onward to connect with the man's body.

The man dropped to the ground, unmoving.

The woman stopped struggling. The banker gaped at the body now beside him on the floor. Everyone running to assist circled around and froze in their tracks. His mother was silent somewhere behind him.

He did it.

"Have you seen it now, Mr. Kamen?"

He had been the one to kill that man.

Four years old.

"Mr. Kamen?"

His focus shifted to the man before him. This man sat

on the sage green sofa facing the front window, causing the glare from outdoors to reflect in the lenses of the man's eyeglasses. The reflection of sunlight obscured his eyes from being seen, as if they were sunglasses. He supposed they were, in fact, glasses of sun, at this moment. He chuckled softly as he inhaled deeply, shaking the cobwebs of the memories aside.

The sight of the sofa brought him fully into the present. It was his favorite sofa, and where most of his reading, researching, and contemplating occurred. Often, he would even nap on that sofa, and he had awakened to find himself stretched out on that sofa when the sun rose through the same window now behind him on more than one occasion.

This was his home.

He looked down at the paper in his hands, a thirty-year-old copy of a newspaper. Its headline proclaimed:

'HOME-WRECKER' CAUGHT
DEAD IN THE ACT

The report below it he had just read told of a serial killer authorities had been tracking for years whose game was deceiving fairly wealthy women until they agreed to marry him. He then promptly forced the women to transfer all funds and anything of value into new accounts before torturing and murdering them, often in front of a video camera, earning him the media nickname of "The Home-wrecker." Copies of each video had arrived by postal mail to various police stations around the country, seemingly at random.

The paper stated the murderer had been at a local bank about to close the deal on his latest victim when he suddenly keeled over for unknown reasons. "An act of God," one witness was reported to declare when the murderer was identified. The woman who narrowly escaped becoming his eleventh victim had declined all requests for interviews.

Inserted to the side of the text was a photo of a man sprawled across a floor. A still shot clearly taken from a security camera, the picture showed many people gathered around the man, frozen in various states of motion, but it was the smallest who now held his attention.

A young boy stood nearest to the man. The boy's right hand was extended in the direction of the man, as if he wanted to help the man back to his feet.

"Forgive me—I should have perhaps begun with something a bit less... disorienting? I apologize..."

"No, no," Audi replied, glancing up. "It's... all right."

He brought the newspaper closer to his face, and peered at the photo. Two hands were reaching for the boy, from behind the boy. The body belonging to the hands was hidden by a man standing between the camera and the owner of the hands. His eyes followed the trail of where the person's arms would lead. A head was visible just above the shoulder of the man in the way, positioned where it was clearly belonging with the hands reaching for the boy.

It was the face of his mother.

Audi stared intently at his mother's face for some time. The man on his sofa patiently and respectfully remained silent.

She had been gone eighteen years now. To see her now, from a strange source, from a strange man, after all these years was... unexpected. To see her so young...

"Where did you get this?" he asked, barely a whisper.

"It was in the collection of a friend of mine. She has passed now, bless her, but," he smiled slightly, "I seem to have caught her passion."

"Her passion?"

"Yes. You see, my friend was a very curious woman. You would struggle to believe the vast amounts of information she collected on particular subjects—entire rooms full of papers, books, and objects. The grandest library pales in comparison!"

Audi merely studied the man, who struggled to contain

his sudden excitement, and appeared to be a bit uncomfortable under his gaze. Audi had returned home from his habitual visit to a nearby wooded area to find this man standing on his porch, a briefcase in his hand, and a grey plaid cap on his head. He seemed familiar somehow, yet he was unable to place in what way. He had been about to ask the man what he wanted when the man had spoken first. "I found you."

The man now motioned to the newspaper again, before pushing his eyeglasses up the bridge of his nose.

"Do you... remember this day?" he asked.

Running his thumb lightly across the photo printed on the yellowing newsprint, he finally nodded. "I had forgotten, though."

The man slapped his own thigh. "I should have known better—I do apologize deeply! I should have shown something else first. My mind tends to be a bit overly logical, I'm afraid." He smiled embarrassedly. "The beginning is not always the best place to start."

"Something else?" Audi's eyes dropped to the briefcase on the cushion beside the man.

"Oh, yes!" He rummaged briefly through the contents of the case before pulling out another photograph and held it up.

Audi's jaw dropped when he saw the image on the eight by ten inch print.

"Who *are* you?"

• CHAPTER 2 •

━━━━━━━━━━━━⟨ ⟩━━━━━━━━━━━━

"OH, I ASSURE YOU," the man said, "I am exactly who I say I am." He set the photo in his lap, then pulled a business card from his inside coat pocket and offered it to Audi. A glint of metallic green foil caught his eye as he accepted it. "You can thoroughly trust me."

"In the movies, if someone has to say such a thing, it always means the opposite."

The man shifted nervously in his seat for a moment before he realized Audi was smiling slightly. He suddenly busied himself rifling through the contents of the briefcase again. Audi noted the behavior silently as he inspected the card.

The green foil was an image of a spider within an equilateral triangle at top center. Horizontal lines of the same shiny green foil extended from the central logo to each edge of the card. Below the image read:

WENDELL JOHNSON
PROFESSIONAL ARCHIVAL SERVICES
PRIVATE AND CONFIDENTIAL

He flipped it over and found a hand-written phone

number, with the words *I can help* written below. Glancing up, he saw Johnson was unmoving again, watching him.

"And where did you get that photo?" Audi asked, motioning.

"Ah, it was also in the collection of my friend. It was included with the newspaper where I found them. I, uh," he held it out to Audi again, "I take it you do know who this is?"

Audi stared at the picture for a long moment. Memories swam past his mind's eye. Places and times that seemed like another life resurfaced to be relived. But it was in this life he knew the girl in the photograph. Her hazel eyes and layered strawberry-blonde hair leaped from the page at him like a dream dancing at the edge of his awareness—remembered, but nearly forgotten. Images previously burned into his mind's eye overlayed with the photo presently in front of him, disorienting his senses for a moment. The small smile she gave the camera stirred both warmth and pain in his heart. He had been very familiar with that smile.

He nodded. "I took this photo."

"You did?" Johnson was unable to hide his surprise. "Well!"

"How did this end up in your friend's collection?"

"Oh I couldn't tell you that, I'm afraid," he pressed his glasses up his nose. "I didn't even know you were the one who snapped it. Quite a small world, eh?"

Audi was not amused. "If you didn't know this was my photo at one time, then how did you know it was associated with me? How did you know that was me in the newspaper, for that matter? The article mentioned nothing about me or…" Audi trailed off.

"Your mother," Johnson whispered.

"Yes."

"I said I did not know you had. Yet my friend clearly did know—she had them in the same file."

"A file on me," he stated suspiciously.

"Well, yes," he confirmed nervously. "As you can see from my card, I am an archivist. My friend enlisted my services some time ago to catalog and maintain her vast collection."

"So, your client then," Audi said. "Who is she?"

"Well, I suppose it could be said I was more her client than the other way around, but by the end, we were also friends." His glasses slid down his nose again, but he made no move to push them up. "She passed these on to me when she... left."

"Only the files on me, or the entire collection?"

"Oh, the whole lot."

"Who was she?" he asked again.

"Well," Johnson began, "She, along with the collection uh, also passed along strict instructions to never reveal her identity."

Audi's intuition was now at high alert. He leaned forward in his armchair. "Why would anyone have a file on me? I only stock shelves and clean floors at the hospital. I've done nothing of interest in either a good or bad way. I keep to myself." He looked from the photograph to the newspaper again. "And now a stranger comes to my home with random pieces of my past?"

"Ah, but you see, I don't believe they are random at all, Mr. Kamen!"

Audi waited for him to continue.

"You see, I have a bit of a knack for details—archivist and all, you know—and I believe these two objects are definitely connected," he smiled almost playfully, forgetting his nervousness for a moment. "But I'm afraid I've withheld a piece of the puzzle from you."

"You've withheld a lot from me," Audi replied, "But go on."

Johnson swallowed before continuing. "You see, it takes one object to know another object. The contrast between the two allows each to be known individually, such as day compared to night, and near versus far.

However, a third object is needed if a relative depth of any sort is to be found—a third dimension!

"And this, I believe," he presented another photograph, "Is the third dimension and connective clue linking the newspaper and the girl."

The image revealed another body sprawled on the floor, its mouth open wide. A young man was bent over the body with one hand placed on its forehead and the other hand on its arm. Light strawberry blonde hair could be seen spilling across the floor behind the young man.

A shock went through Audi's system.

Unlike the photo in the newspaper, this picture had clearly not been taken by a security camera, but by a professional—someone who knew what they were doing with a camera. But that fact was not what shocked Audi. What caught him by surprise was the existence of the photo itself. This had happened in a private home, and there had been no one else around.

"Is that not the same girl?" asked Johnson proudly.

"Mr. Johnson," Audi replied calmly but firmly, "Why are you here?"

The archivist broke into a broad grin and clapped his hands together sharply. "So it's true! It *is* you—and you know exactly what I'm getting at here!" He leaned forward. "It seems you *have* done things of interest after all, Mr. Kamen. That is what I'm interested in."

"I think it's time for you to go," Audi said, rising.

"And do you know what else I think?"

"No, and frankly, I don't care." Audi stood. "Please leave now, Mr. Johnson."

"I think the two are connected—what happened in the newspaper, and what happened with the girl." Johnson remained planted on the sofa. "Do you know what I'm talking about, Mr. Kamen?"

"You have intruded—"

"To give and to take, Mr. Kamen! To give and to take!"

Audi stared at him, speechless.

"That *is* what you're doing to the girl there, isn't it?"

"I have no idea what you are talking about, and have asked you to leave."

Johnson closed the briefcase and stood as Audi herded him toward the door.

"Do you know where she is, Mr. Kamen?"

Audi froze. "What?" he asked.

"Do you know where Rachel is?"

Audi could only stare at him.

"I talked to her," Johnson said smugly. "The girl in the photo. I met with her." He leaned in a bit to whisper, "She's even more beautiful now, you know."

Audi's mind raced. The past was forever separated and distant, yet forever as close as yesterday inside. Ten years was a long time, but always available, no matter how hard one tried to forget. He steeled his determination that this conversation was now over.

"What does an archivist want with a person's private life? Merely expanding the collection? I think you should stick to alphabetizing what already exists."

"What happened with her, Mr. Kamen?"

"I don't know what sort of business your 'friend' was into, or why my personal privacy has been violated, but I strongly suggest you leave my property right now, Mr. Johnson, before I decide I need to call the authorities."

The momentary boldness Johnson had found evaporated in an instant, and was replaced by his previous nervousness. A trace of fear shot through his eyes.

"Mr. Kamen…"

"Goodbye, Mr. Johns—"

"She's looking for you!" Johnson spoke over him. Audi paused. "I already knew where you lived, but I did not violate your privacy. I didn't tell her where you were."

Audi allowed a stretch of silence before speaking.

"Why would she want to see me again?"

"She's perfectly fine, Audi," he answered softly. "Better than ever, in fact. She understands now."

"It seems you know much more of what happened, or what you think happened, than you pretend to."

Johnson bowed his head and closed his eyes as he took a deep breath.

"I shall leave you to your business. I thank you very much for your time. Please remember I would very much like to speak with you in greater length about these things—when you are ready, and, of course, when it is more convenient timing for you."

He crossed the porch, then turned once more. "Oh, and that number on the back of my card? I did not write that. Do not call it, unless you are one thousand percent positive you are ready to… explore these things.

"In the meantime, I will contact you again. Good afternoon, Mr. Kamen."

Johnson smiled, then walked away.

• CHAPTER 3 •

A SIGH INVOLUNTARILY ESCAPED her lips as she skimmed the printed script. Although the studio provided everyone with a copy, she was the only one she knew who read it at all before going live. The others saw it as a waste of time—the words would scroll on the teleprompter, so why bother reading the paper too?

An obvious reason she reviewed the stories being covered was to acquaint herself with the material before trying to speak it aloud in front of one-point-two million people.

Another reason was to brace herself for the broadcast's nightly barrage of negativity. Channel seven was the only station boasting one anchorperson per show. The director claimed it was less disorienting than switching back and forth between two newscasters, and provided the audience with a more intimate experience. It also placed the entire load of negativity solely on her shoulders, with no one to half it with.

There's something seriously wrong when I have to desensitize myself before I'm able to perform my job.

She sighed again audibly.

A quick knock at her open door snapped her from her

thoughts. She looked up quickly.

"On in ten, Sav."

"Oh thanks, Phil." Scooping up her papers, she tapped them on the desktop, straightening them to perfection.

Five years at the news desk had more than taken their toll on her mind and energy, when they were supposed to have done the opposite for her. It had managed to work its way so deep it was now affecting her body. Each morning it was more and more difficult to get out of bed, and it was not simply because she no longer enjoyed the job. She felt the deeper layers of herself bogged down by the depressing nature of her duties.

Why had she gotten into this line of work again? Drama and negativity sapped her vitality like a leach. It was like growing up with her parents all over again.

She paused in front of the mirror to check her hair and makeup. They were still good, though her eyebrows were noticeably more knit than they had ever been before. They were also now slightly upturned, giving her face a saddened appearance.

I look like my cat just died, she sighed. *What great camera candy I am—not even thirty yet, and already wearing down.* She flashed a test smile at herself. Her face stretched and masked most of the weariness. She raised her eyebrows and winked.

Sigh.

Emerging from her dressing room, she was immediately surrounded by the familiar behind-the-scenes sounds of the production studio. Aides rushed to and fro, straining to hear the orders from their superiors over the racket of pre-air newscast preparations, and dodged other aides, employees, and equipment as they excitedly earned their foot-in-the-door break into the business, as well as their paycheck. The mingled scents of sweat, grease, perfume, and electric heat barely registered to her, but her nose still wrinkled and tickled every time she left the safety of the potpourri environment she had created in her own little office.

She inhaled a deep breath, then blew it out quickly, shifting toward professional mode.

"Hi, Miss Marcus, you look more beautiful than ever today! Get you anything last minute?"

She turned to the young man who had followed her around every day for the last ten months, though he was actually the aide to one of the cameramen. He had developed such a schoolboy crush on her that he was willing to wear himself out making sure she was taken care of.

"Hi, Lance," she smiled at him as he turned his daily shade of red in response. He couldn't have been more than a month or two out of high school when he came to work at the station. A flash of guilt sparked in her as she realized she had never taken the time to ask anything about him really. "As always, I'm just fine. Thank you though!"

"No problem at all, Miss Marcus—and I mean that! It really would be no problem at all for me, you know, if you ever need any special errands or favors!"

She smiled again as she rounded the anchor desk and took her chair. "I know, Lance."

"Two minutes," her earpiece said as she fit it in place. Lance ducked off set and disappeared somewhere into the darkness behind the cameras.

She arranged her papers and glanced at the top story once more. Another prisoner had broken out of the local penitentiary again. *Again,* she sighed. *What is wrong with this place?*

"And ten, nine, eight…"

The red ON AIR light came on.

"Good evening, Friends! I'm Savannah Marcus, and this is your evening report." She flashed the trademark smile that had won her three awards already. "Thank you for joining me!

"Tonight, we want to begin by urging extreme caution. Authorities are again extensively searching the city for a

Stephens County Detention Center inmate who escaped earlier this afternoon. Twenty-seven year old Carl Walcott is serving thirty years for the attempted murder of previous mayoral hopeful John Bridges four years ago. This is the local prison's third breakout in the last two years. How the escape was accomplished remains unknown at this time. Police encourage all residents—"

Fire suddenly erupted in her left shoulder.

A tremendous noise registered in her ears as she was thrown from the chair she had sat in for five years. Black clouds swam quickly into her vision, blotting out the hot, powerful studio lights from the edges inward.

The lights abruptly grew brighter and overpowered the black clouds. The light was so bright and glaring she had to squint. Someone had switched on the overhead house lights. Why were the house lights up? The show had just started; she wasn't done yet! How did she fall out of her chair? *What graceful camera candy.*

She could hear people shouting, and what sounded like metal slamming onto the floor. Another loud noise echoed around her, but the black clouds were enclosing the light once again. Faces appeared over her. *Get off the set, I'm still on live!*

Her shoulder hurt. Why was everyone rushing around? The show just started. Turn the house lights off! Wait— were they still on? It was so dark now. It was so, so dark.

Her ears were ringing. What *is* that noise? Oh my God, make it stop! What is that squealing?

She sat up and looked around. Everyone had left. The set was dark and no one was around her anymore. She quickly realized her ears were not ringing from a piercing sound, but from a piercing *lack* of sound.

And her shoulder didn't hurt anymore.

She slowly rotated her arm, testing the muscles that had been on fire only moments ago.

"Hello?" she called out as she struggled to her feet, still holding her shoulder. No answer returned.

She looked around the abandoned set. All lights were now off, all cameras and projectors powered down. Even the hallway to the right of the news set was dark—something she had never seen in the twenty-four hour, three hundred and sixty-five days a year television station before.

But there was a light on somewhere. It seemed to be more of a soft glow than a full bulb-light, like some sort of back-up generator emergency lighting. Most emergency lighting she had seen was a sickly green hue, but this was a gentle, pleasing blue-white.

Savannah gradually made her way around the edge of the news desk, toward the light. Stepping down from the platform, her feet habitually performed their familiar motions around cables, cords, and monitors. *Does it mean I've been in one place too long when I can maneuver a place even in darkness?*

As she made her way around the largest main camera, the source of the light came into view. She stopped walking and stared at the object. At first, her brain did not register what she was looking at, but then slowly made sense of the image.

A tree.

A tree in the center of the studio?

A *glowing* tree?

She twisted to look around the entire room again. "What is going on here?" she asked aloud. No one answered her question.

Turning back to the tree, she found it was closer to her than it had been a moment ago. Was it moving? Crouching slightly, she squinted her eyes at the tree, trying to gauge whether it was standing still or not.

Her toe stubbed on a large coil of cables, but she felt no pain. It was she who had been moving toward the tree, and she had lost her shoes. Had she even had them on? Yes, she had just begun her evening broadcast.

The tree captured her full attention once again as she continued stepping toward it. It was so warm and inviting, as if it were drawing her in, beckoning, offering her a peace she wasn't sure she had ever felt in her life.

All concerns about her broadcast, what had happened to the station, where everyone had gone, and what was even going on now began to fade from her mind as she drew near the tree.

She saw it was not the tree itself that glowed, but rather thousands of strange symbols carved into its entire surface. Were the symbols themselves glowing, or was it the internal wood of the tree now exposed that radiated the blue-white glow? Either way, it was thoroughly captivating.

Savannah realized she was smiling as she cautiously extended a hand to touch the tree.

Oh my God...

She held her palm to the trunk of the tree, unable to break from the sensation it passed up her arm to the rest of her body. The utter calmness that encompassed her was beyond ecstatic. The journalist in her who typically never lacked for words was completely speechless and grinning like a fool.

Before she realized she was even moving, she had pressed the entire length of her body to the tree, trying to get as much contact with it possible. A deep sigh exhaled from her core, draining every ounce of tension from her body. A giggle escaped her lips as she closed her eyes and fully wrapped her arms and legs around the base of the tree in total relaxation.

Anything else no longer mattered.

Abruptly, the impression of falling dawned on her senses.

She opened her eyes and found she was sliding down the tree as if it were the pole of a firefighter. Her arms and legs seemed to have become a part of the tree, merging as one with its trunk. Savannah realized her downward motion was more of an integrated moving *with* the tree than it was a separate sliding, as she would slide down a pole, yet she felt no fear or panic as she descended. Wasn't it natural to be a part of the tree itself? Hadn't she been connected to it this way her entire life?

The studio floated up and away from her. She smiled dreamily as she passed through the floor and continued downward.

What seemed to be the tops of more trees came into view below her, and Savannah saw this was indeed the case as she reached them and continued into their midst.

Each tree of this subterranean forest also bore the foreign symbols and carvings, yet each glowed a different color. Soft and soothing greens, oranges, yellows, and purples emanated as far as her eyes could see in all directions—a rainbow of ecstasy, as each also emitted the same euphoric sensations. She felt it to her bones.

Her legs and arms came apart from her tree as she reached the surface. She turned around, and slid her back down the trunk until she was sitting on the ground. The sensations from the tree were warm against her spine, soothing like an organic heating pad.

Savannah happily turned her head this way and that, absorbing the astonishing pastel visuals surrounding her, and soaking in the rejuvenating vibrations she now realized came from the ground as well as the trees. She no longer cared about anything anywhere else.

A bare thread of thought zipped through her mind: *What is this place?* Then it was gone in the same split second.

Two large blue symbols glowed on a particularly huge tree to her left. These two above all seemed to hold her eyes. She rested her head back against her own tree as she stared at the two symbols, then sat up with a start as she realized they were not symbols at all, but two large blue eyes she was staring into.

The air around the massive tree slowly began to wave. The wave grew into a shimmer, increasing in both speed and density. It gradually grew more and more opaque, until it was nearly a solid white, shaping itself into a form. Her eyes and mind struggled to make sense of the shape the air was taking.

A wolf.

Savannah gasped as the wolf materialized before her, though her body and mind never left the state of total relaxation. As with descending the tree, she felt no fear, when a rational mind would normally have been terrified.

The wolf separated from the tree, took four steps toward her, then stopped and sat perfectly still, merely watching her. Was it as surprised to see her there as she was to be there? Should she get up and run? Try to climb back up the tree? Stay as motionless as possible?

She smiled at the wolf. It seemed to smile at her in return, but Savannah was not sure how she knew it was smiling—nothing in its physical features changed; the faint luminescence around its entire body remained steady.

But it was smiling at her.

She leaned her head back against the tree again. *This is so nice. Why haven't I ever come here before?*

Noises began to enter her awareness. Sounds from the trees all around her suddenly seemed louder, where they had been virtually nonexistent before. Had they been silent, or had she simply not noticed them? She had never heard any sounds like these—a combination of bird song, mouse chatter, cat purr, and breathing lungs all at once. It was an odd and indefinable mixture with a consistent rhythm to it. The result was nowhere near unpleasant; it was actually quite melodious and enjoyable. Were the trees making the sounds, or were there more animals like the wolf in or around the trees?

Turning her attention back to the enormous white wolf sitting perfectly motionless before her, Savannah felt it was still smiling at her. Its blue eyes were fixed directly on her eyes.

As she watched, it shifted its eyes, dropped its gaze slightly, and then raised its eyes to meet her own once again. She smiled. Was it shy?

The wolf repeated the process twice more, then took another step toward her. It raised its front right paw toward her. Holding its paw in the air, it looked her in the eyes once more, as if questioning.

She smiled at it again.

It lowered its gaze, shook its paw slightly, and looked at her.

Is it trying to tell me something? Is it actually trying to communi—

Savannah's thoughts broke off as one part of the wolf's paw began to stretch and thin. The edge of the paw changed its shape until it resembled a finger.

A human finger.

It was pointing at her!

The wolf dropped its gaze to where it was pointing. Savannah lowered her eyes to follow, and gasped.

Her left shoulder was gaping open again.

She leapt to her feet and clamped her palm over the wound. Something really had happened, hadn't it? What had she been doing again? Lying down. No—sitting! She had been sitting at her desk, the news desk. Then she had lain on the floor. And her shoulder had hurt then, hadn't it? Why had it hurt?

A soft pressure on the back of her hand made her look down to find the wolf was now directly beside her. It had placed its paw on her hand, and was looking her in the eye again. She could easily get lost in those eyes, so deep, so... pure. She felt no reason to fear at all from them.

When it saw it had her attention again, it turned its head toward the large tree it had materialized from. The wolf tapped her hand twice, then pointed its eerie human finger at the tree. When she made no movement, the wolf went over to the tree and sat beside it, facing her again.

Savannah slowly took a step forward, her hand still over her injury. The wolf smiled and dipped its head, encouraging her.

She drew near the tree, and saw the two large blue

symbols that the wolf's eyes had emerged from were still on the tree. Inside was a thick and glowing sap-like fluid, swirling slowly. As the sap worked itself around and around, it oozed out of the holes little by little. The wolf watched it creep out, smiling.

When enough sap had emerged, it dipped its finger-paw in the midst of it and turned to Savannah. Slowly extending its arm, it carefully began applying the sap to her wound.

Savannah braced for her body to flinch in reaction, but it never came. No pain entered her awareness, even as the wolf pressed its finger deeper into the wound. It occurred to her the wound had not actually hurt even when she first realized she was injured.

The sap produced a tingling sensation that quickly spread down her back, chest, and arm. As the tingling began running down her legs, it seemed to intensify into a searing, as if a hot branding iron were being applied to her entire body. Yet it was not pain it created in her body, but a pleasure running deeper than Savannah had ever felt before—far beyond any orgasmic experience she had ever reached, including at her own hand.

The sounds in the forest grew still again as the wolf applied a second layer of the glowing salve to her wound. The sound of rushing water broke the silence just as her legs buckled out from under her, and she collapsed to the soft, spongy ground. She felt an incredible warmth covering every centimeter of her body. Her lips were spread in a wide smile as she soaked in the experience of whatever the wolf had done to her.

She opened her eyes, having no memory she had even closed them.

The searing and tingling had completely stopped. Had they stopped abruptly, or had it been gradually? Had she fallen asleep? The light of this place looked no different than before, but she had had no sense of time here before either.

Lifting her head, she saw the wolf was nowhere to be

seen. The two blue symbols in the trunk of the huge tree were merely symbols again, and not sap-oozing holes. She twisted to look back at the tree she had slid down. It appeared to be the same, except a great red circle was now glowing toward the left side of it, at nearly head height. Had that been there before?

She cautiously stood to her feet, moving slowly in case she grew dizzy or nauseous. Stretching her arms wide, she realized she actually felt quite well—very strong and healthy. She took a deep breath, and blew it out slowly. A tingle similar to what she had felt with the sap rolled through her body, and she felt even better. She repeated the breath as an experiment, and smiled again as she found it had the same effect once more.

Savannah also found the wound on her shoulder had disappeared. No trace of scarring or any sign there had ever been a wound there remained.

What in the world did that wolf do to me?

She moved to her tree, and leaned in close to examine the red circle. She suddenly gasped, and stepped back.

The glowing red circle seemed to be at the same height the wound on her shoulder had been!

She stood up straight and stepped closer, measuring. The circle was placed at an exact mirroring to her left shoulder, where her wound had been.

Savannah leaned forward, placing her weight against the tree while her mind raced, pondering everything that had happened to her here today, if it had been only one day, and what all of it could mean.

The soft pulling sensation tugged at her body, and she gave in to it without hesitation. She wrapped her arms and legs around the tree as she allowed it to take her as part of itself once again. The movement began sliding her up the tree this time, in the same way she had come down.

Darkness grew deeper and deeper the higher she ascended, but still she relaxed into the movement. When it was too dark to see, she simply closed her eyes. She began to hear a faint beeping sound, repeating steadily and consistently. She thought she heard voices intermingled, but could not be sure.

Gradually, the darkness began to take on a dim shade of gray. The gray grew brighter, until it was a vivid glow that did not even begin to compare with the glow of the trees she had just left behind. The glow grew brighter still until it became a full light.

She slowly opened her eyes.

"Well, well, well," said a voice to her right. "Miss Marcus! Welcome back to earth!"

The light was still too bright for her to make definite sense of anything, but she turned toward the voice.

"Who... who are you?" she asked roughly, her voice refusing to fully cooperate. "Where am I?"

A hand patted her arm gently. "You're all right now. We got you back. You're safe. You're in South Grace Hospital. You gave us all a real good scare there, you know—

"You died on us."

• CHAPTER 4 •

━━━━━━━━━━━━━━━━━━━━━━━━━**◦( )◦**━━━━━━━━━━━━━━━━━━━

WHEN THE ELEVATOR BUZZED to announce he had arrived, Audi jumped. Why maintenance had selected a mind-jolting buzz instead of a soft chime or ding like most elevators was beyond him. Maybe he would take it upon himself one day to just replace it. He did his best thinking during the abnormally slow elevator rides between assignments—his best thinking at work, anyway. Audi's truly deep thinking was done in the woods near his home. His second place was lounging on his green sofa, staring out the window.

His scattered train of thoughts began to settle back into place as he exited the elevator. He shoved his utility cart to the left and down the hallway.

Mr. Johnson's visit the day before had rattled him more than he cared to admit. He had barely slept at all that night, and had only been able to sigh when he saw the list of orders waiting for him upon arrival at work. It seemed all twenty-two floors had called in replenish orders. The number of patients admitted was clearly at a record high; he had just made full rounds a few days ago.

He pulled his passkey card up as he reached the supply room of the twenty-second floor, his first stop. The familiar *whir* as its retractable cord extended was soothing to him in a way. He supposed it was simply the comfort of routine; the noise was not particularly pleasing in itself, but it always seemed to help, especially when his mind was cluttered and he was trying to process something.

The image before his mind's eye this time was a snapshot of that photograph in the old newspaper. He had been only four years old at the time, yet still remembered it clearly. Time, and the effort of distraction had slipped it into a back pocket of his mind, but the stranger on his doorstep had brought it all back to the surface in a heartbeat.

He hadn't expected to see it physically before him though. He hadn't known it had made the paper, much less the front page. Another grace his mother had protected him from all these years, it seemed.

Audi maneuvered his supply cart into the narrow room, carefully avoiding upsetting the number of freestanding mops, brooms, and cleaning cloths stacked just inside the door for quick and easy access whenever emergency called for them. In his opinion, the cloths especially should be secured higher, on a shelf or something, yet the supply room of every floor was arranged exactly the same. Maybe he would take that improvement upon himself, as well.

What had happened that day in the bank? His adult mind demanded answers, and looked back at the event's memories in the light of thirty years of life experience.

The woman's screaming was what raised the hairs on the back of his neck most. He had not heard any scream like that since, though he unexplainably knew he had heard it before that day in the bank. Audi had always felt older than his body actually was, as if he knew he had lived previous lives. Had he had that feeling before hearing that scream, or was it the scream that triggered the feeling and sense of déjà vu? He had never found any answers for that. He had technically also avoided seeking answers to that.

Audi slowly ran his finger down the list of supplies

twenty-two had ordered. He always started his deliveries on the highest floor and worked his way down. It felt more organized that way, and was the same way he dusted his home—from the top down, so that nothing he cleaned after something else re-dusted what he had already cleaned. It made sense to him to do his restocking the same way.

The woman had never opened her mouth. No one else had been able to hear the blood-curdling screams coming from her. He had been the only one.

He stuffed boxes of gauze pads into their place on the shelf as he pondered. He had heard the scream inside his head. That was the only explanation, and he knew it was possible. He had heard accounts of others who could "hear" things, but he had never read any accounts of hearing screams.

One thing he did know, even more so now that he was grown and looking back, was that that was the day he had shut the Hearing down within himself. It had been the first and last time he had experienced it, though he *had* explored other forms of that sort of thing. That day had frightened him so badly he never wanted to experience such a thing again—neither the screaming, nor what he had done to the man.

Now, he felt that same edginess pressing in on him. Mr. Johnson had resurrected the memories of that day at four years old, as well as the other incident that had caused him to shut down to the Touching. Johnson had known about both, and had strongly suggested there was a connection between the two.

Audi wasn't sure which scared him more in this moment—the fact strangers had been watching him and knew about these things, or the matter of the things themselves. He had spent the majority of his life hiding from them himself. Maybe that's why he now hid in supply closets for a living.

He finished his work order for this supply, and made his way back to the elevator. Twenty-one had ordered only syringes, gloves, and tissue paper for the patient's restrooms. It would be a quick trip before heading on to the twentieth floor and their longer list.

Audi's mother, Sara, had known what he was able to do. She had never spoken about it with him, or to anyone else that he was aware of, but he knew she knew. The same simple knowing he used to determine if she was telling him the entire truth of a matter or not also told him that she knew.

When he was nine years old, he had found a stack of books hidden in the back of her closet. Most of the pictures on the covers and in the pages had shown naked or half-naked people smeared with all colors of paint. What objects they did wear seemed to be bones, skins, and feathers of various animals. He had learned about American Indians in school, and he knew the people in these books were similar, yet somehow different. Almost all the people's eyes were closed, and they were surrounded by huge fires, drums, and smoke in nearly every photograph.

Not all the books had been that way though. One book had shown images of fully dressed men and women in more modern buildings. The men wore full suits and ties, and the women wore long dresses that reached their feet. The images in those books depicted the people sitting beside or leaning over other people lying in hospital beds or wheelchairs. What had imprinted into his memory from those images was the way each of the people had their hands on the sick or injured person, visibly concentrating intently on what they were doing.

Two words from that book had also stayed in his memory: *Faith Healer.*

Audi braced for the assaulting buzz of the elevator as he arrived at the twenty-first floor. The doors slid open, and he shoved his cart forward. The layout had been designed the same on each floor, so he habitually turned his utility cart to the left.

He suddenly stopped short, and struggled to bring the

momentum of his cart to a halt. Frowning, he studied the neon orange highway cones and security guard blocking his way.

"Charles?"

"Hey, Aud," the guard replied.

"What's going on?" In five years of working at the hospital, he had never seen a section of rooms blocked and guarded. He was used to seeing Charles around the grounds of the building, and couldn't remember a time he had even seen him indoors.

"You haven't heard? That reporter lady on the news— you know Savannah Marcus on channel seven?—she was shot, right on live TV! All kinds of people been trying to get in here to see her, but they're being extra careful about all that, you know, her being a celebrity and all."

"She was shot?"

"Yeah! Right as she was starting her newscast, you know? A damn shame, and a sad world when even a TV station ain't safe from loonies, you know?" Charles shook his head and rolled his eyes skyward.

An image of Savannah Marcus wafted through Audi's mind as he digested this news. Her dark hair and bright blue eyes had always captured his attention on the rare occasions he actually watched the news. "Is she going to make it?" he asked.

"Oh yeah, see that's the other part of why so many people are trying to get in here now—" the security guard spread his arm out as a woman rounded the corner behind Audi and approached. "Oh, I'm sorry, ma'am, I'm afraid I can't let anyone past this point."

"What?" said the woman. "But isn't the ladies room over here?"

"Yes, ma'am," Charles answered, "But I'm afraid you'll have to head up or down a floor and use those commodes. This section is closed for privacy."

"What's going on back there?"

"Oh, nothing to be concerned about, ma'am. Don't

worry one bit."

The woman made a quiet *hmph*, and headed for the elevators.

When the woman was far enough away, Charles leaned in closer to Audi. "So, the reason so many people are trying to get in here now is on account of what happened *after* she got shot."

Audi frowned slightly. "After?"

Charles nodded. "Word is, she died near right away. Right there at the desk, and all on camera!"

"But you said she was going to be all right?"

"Aud, man," the guard nearly whispered, "She *is* all right! Came back, good as new! Not even pain from the gunshot, they say—course I haven't seen for myself, you know. But that's what everyone's saying, and they got me inside here, so to me, that's pretty hard proof right there!"

Audi glanced down the hall past Charles. "Why would they not just post you at her room then? Why rope off this whole block of rooms?"

Charles shrugged. "Don't think there's anyone else in those other rooms. They just gave her the whole block. Maybe they're studying her, trying to figure out how she's still alive."

"This is very unusual," Audi mused. "Well, the supply closet I have orders for is over there. Can I fill my order?"

The security guard shook his head. "Sorry, Aud. They said nobody goes in."

"Even employees?"

"Yup."

"But you know me, Charles," Audi pressed. "I've only got a few things to deliver—I'll be right in and out. I hate leaving work undone."

Charles looked uncertain. "Well, I don't know, you know? I really can't get in trouble, man. Jackie has already been after me to ask about a raise. I can't risk going the opposite way, and get myself fired instead—she'd have my hide!"

Audi nodded. "All right, I understand." He turned and looked down the hall behind him. Nobody was in sight. "But you're already on that side. Could you take my supplies down there for me, if I watch the front here for you? That way wouldn't be going against orders."

"Well, I don't know…"

"It's only these three things here, and you wouldn't even have to find where they go—just stick them inside the door there so anyone looking for what they ordered will find them, okay?"

"Well," Charles looked very nervous, "That's all?"

Audi nodded and smiled.

"Well, all right. You'll stay right here and not let anyone pass, right?"

"Right."

Charles slowly took the box of syringe tubes, box of gloves, and case of tissue paper, then hurried down the hall and around the corner to the supply room.

Admitting to himself that he was more curious about Savannah Marcus being here than he was about getting his supplies delivered, Audi immediately checked behind himself again before quickly slipping past the security cones. A part of him was extremely curious what had happened to her, as his deceit with Charles revealed.

He peered into the first room, figuring the room closest to where security had been posted was the one Savannah had been admitted to. It had clearly held a patient recently, but the room had not been remade or cleaned.

Audi frowned at the lapse in hospital policy as he hurried to the next room, aware it wouldn't take his friend long at all to return.

The next room was empty as well, but cleaned and prepared for the next patient. He looked to the corner Charles had disappeared around. This was already taking too much time.

An idea suddenly occurred to him. Something from the recesses of his memory surfaced, perhaps brought on by the recent waves Johnson had caused. A flicker of hesitation followed. Would he even be able to do it? Should he? He hadn't even tried such a thing since—he cut that thought short, redirecting it from thinking about *her*. He needed to decide fast—he was running out of time.

Audi decided he would.

He closed his eyes and inhaled a deep breath. He brought to mind an image of the Savannah Marcus presented on the television each evening, then simultaneously visualized the layout of this floor. In his mind, he slid the two images on top of each other and projected the inquiring intention of *Find Savannah*.

Nothing happened.

Inhaling another breath, he tried again. *Find Savannah*.

He opened his eyes. Could he not do that trick anymore? Had he lost it from mere lack of use over the years?

He closed his eyes again. *Find Charles*.

A slight jolt, almost like a small electric shock poked his mind in the space just outside the supply room of his mental map. The trick still worked for him just fine. It also told him that Charles was on his way back. Time was almost up.

On a whim, he expanded his mental map to include the entire hospital. *Find Savannah*.

Nothing.

She was not in this building.

He hurried back to the side of the security cones he was supposed to be on just before Charles hurried into view.

"Nothing happened?" the security guard asked.

An alarm rocketed through Audi for a split second. How could Charles have known what he had tried? He realized there was no way he could have known as the internal alarm melted away, and he understood Charles had meant something else.

"No, didn't see a soul."

The guard's shoulders seemed to drop five inches as he

visibly relaxed and nodded in relief.

"Hey, thanks again for getting those in there for me," Audi said as he turned his cart around. "I owe you one!"

Charles waved his hand in dismissal of the thanks, though he continued to glance around nervously as Audi pressed the button to call the elevator.

Why had he not been able to locate Savannah Marcus? He knew she was here, or was supposed to be here. Had they moved her in secret, leaving this hospital as a decoy for the people wanting to reach her?

As the elevator buzzed open for him at the twentieth floor, Audi thought about how he had been able to use the locating trick again, even after so much time had passed. It had come very naturally, and felt as if he had never stopped using it. The trick had been useful to him in even more things than locating someone or something, as he had done with Rachel.

Rachel.

Audi sighed as he shoved his supply cart down the hall and cursed Wendell Johnson. He could feel prickles on his neck from the floodgates that had been and were about to be opened with all this. As far as he was concerned, the past needed to stay just that—the past.

"Such a can of worms," he grumbled as he nearly crashed into a woman rushing out of a room to his right.

Dark hair flew in front of the woman's face and back down again as her hands gripped the edge of his cart to keep from falling. Wide, blue eyes met his as she looked up, more startled than she already clearly had been as she ran from the room. She wore a hospital gown underneath one of the thin robes with the South Grace logo at the breast the hospital provided its patients.

It was Savannah Marcus.

• CHAPTER 5 •

THE WIND HOWLED AT her back as she stepped through the curtain around the bed. Or was it the wolf that was howling? Could it even make audible sounds at all?

The woman lying in the bed before her was clearly having difficulty breathing. Numerous monitors and machines beeped and whirred as various cords and tubes trailed from her body to the machines. Her eyes were closed, and she appeared to be unaware she had a visitor.

The wind abruptly stopped blowing. How there had been wind in the first place would only occur to her as she reflected on this experience later.

Turning to the wolf beside her, she was surprised to find it a distance back, sitting at the foot of the tree again. Had it made any sound at all as it moved? She glanced back to the woman before walking to the wolf and tree. The wolf in turn looked to the tree, then back to her. She saw the tree was oozing its glowing sap once again.

Savannah instantly twisted her neck to check her shoulder. It was perfectly fine, looking as if nothing had ever happened to it, just as the doctors and nurses who had prodded and probed her endlessly had said. They had all been in states of complete shock and wonder. A miracle, they said.

She wouldn't have believed it herself, if it weren't for her own memory of being thrown out of her broadcast chair and feeling fire in her shoulder. It was funny how pure pain could feel like fire—an element completely separate from a human body, as if the pain were something happening outside, and not inside her nervous system.

And how *had* she healed?

In her memory, a shimmering wolf in a surreal world had directed her to put radioactive-looking goop from a tree into her wound, which had knocked her unconscious. Then she had found herself in the hospital.

That had to have all been side effects from whatever drugs they had given her, didn't it? None of that had been real.

But that still did not explain her miraculous recovery.

And if she was now perfectly fine, why had they pumped her full of the psychotropic drugs again? She hadn't even been in any sort of pain, yet she had awoken in her hospital room, alone, and again seen the glowing tree at the foot of her bed. Its mysterious and lustrously carved symbols had illuminated her hands as she found herself unable to resist reaching out to touch its surface.

All thoughts of the experience being residual effects from her first dose of the drugs had evaporated as her fingertips determined the tree was definitely real.

As if on cue, the wolf had materialized from the tree, nearly beneath her hand. She had jumped back, startled. The wolf had simply smiled its impossible smile, and wrapped its paws around the tree. It had looked at her as it slid-moved down the trunk as she had imagined she'd done before, clearly beckoning her.

Savannah had glanced to the silent hallway before following. She had known they had been turning away the media and other visitors who were curious about her miraculous recovery, sheltering her while the attending doctors and professionals ran every test they could think of

THE HEALER • 57

to figure out exactly what had happened themselves—had the higher-ups now barred even the doctors from seeing her? She had felt partly relieved, partly uneasy at that thought.

Of course, if she was only hallucinating again, she may not have been alone at all, but could have been surrounded by a dozen people for all she knew.

Slipping down the tree had seemed to be even easier for her this time, and she hadn't felt the momentary disorientation. She hadn't felt as if she were falling at all. It had felt as natural as if she were simply moving the muscles of her arms and legs to walk—no conscious thought about moving passed her awareness; she simply moved down the tree.

What *had* given her pause was finding no multi-colored forest at the bottom of the tree as she had before. She had expected to come to the soothing tones of the trees, and had realized that the thought of being in that forest again had actually been her motivation for moving down the tree again—she wanted to be there!

When she had instead found just another hospital room, she had been very disappointed. Was disappointment a normal sort of thing to experience during hallucinations? Were expectations and emotions always this realistic feeling?

Discovering the woman inside the bed curtains had dispelled her rambling thoughts and sadness instantly.

Now, from her place beside the wolf and tree, Savannah glanced at the woman in the bed again, and froze.

Wafts of smoke seemed to be rising from the woman's entire body, as if she were slow-burning. Savannah momentarily panicked and rushed to the bedside to look for actual flames, but found none. She leaned closer, and found the smoke was coming out of the woman's pores, as if something inside was leaking from her.

The ghostly wolf merely sat by the tree, watching her. It gave her no indication what was expected of her this time, other than its drawing her attention to the presence of the sap.

If she was fine, and this woman was not, did it expect her to apply the sap to the woman? It was apparently what had healed her shoulder, but would it help whatever this woman was suffering from as well? What caused leaky pore syndrome? The wolf continued to simply look at her as she chuckled at her own diagnostic description.

She felt bad for the woman, whoever she was. It seemed the same heart-wrenching urge she had felt for years over the course of her career was active even here in this hallucinogenic world. The same internal need to take care of or fix each hurt and mistreated person or animal she had reported on now throbbed in her chest as she watched this woman suffer.

What could it hurt to try? None of this was real anyway.

Savannah scooped a handful of the sap into her palm and returned to the woman. She took the wolf's joining her as a sign she had decided to do the correct thing.

With her upturned palm of ooze hovering over the woman, Savannah hesitated.

Where exactly did the woman need the salve placed? No physical injuries were visible, the way her shoulder had been. The woman was clearly suffering internally. Did the smoking pores need to be plugged with the sap? Should she cover the woman's entire body?

Suddenly, the wolf jumped completely onto the bed. It placed one huge paw on the woman's forehead, then turned to Savannah. She was about to begin placing the sap on the woman's forehead where it had indicated when the wolf abruptly touched its other paw to the center of her own forehead.

Savannah gasped as the woman's entire body lit up. The woman's form seemed to be shaped entirely of the wispy smoke, which now shimmered as the wolf's form did. She saw the wafts of smoke were not leaking from the woman's pores as it had seemed, but were generally leaking from her entire essence—the woman was essentially evaporating bit by bit!

A single dark spot on the woman's stomach drew Savannah's attention, a solitary difference in her smoke-body. She leaned forward to examine the dark spot, and her head slipped from the wolf's touch.

The woman's body unexpectedly snapped back to a solid form of flesh.

Savannah covered her mouth in surprise, and looked to the wolf. It seemed to be smiling again as it held its paw to her forehead once more.

The woman's body lit.

Savannah released the breath she hadn't realized she was holding, and slowly moved closer to the dark spot, thinking it must be the ever-curious journalist's blood in her that accepted what was happening and what she was seeing without freaking out. Or, again, maybe this was simply how everyone handled hallucinations while in the middle of experiencing them. She had been too focused on her education and career to give much time to the usual college antics that may have otherwise provided her with a basis to relate this to.

She noticed the movement of the woman's smoke-body was coagulating around the dark spot, and being sucked inside it like a tornado. The smoke was then being shoved out the sides of the spot in every direction. Following the trail of the ejected smoke, Savannah saw this was actually the smoke that was wafting upwards. Once the dark spot spit the smoke back out, the smoke traveled along the surface of the woman's body a bit, and then seemed to break loose altogether and float away.

Understanding flooded her system—the spot was leeching the woman! That must be the source of her suffering.

The wolf seemed to sense her understanding as well, and removed its paws from their foreheads. The woman's body changed back to flesh and bone.

Without hesitation, Savannah raised the woman's gown and slapped the blue tree sap onto her belly where she had seen the spot. The woman instantly screamed and sat bolt upright.

Savannah jumped back, her open mouth mirroring the woman's shrieking mouth.

The woman's eyes were now wide open, though they stared blindly ahead, unseeing. Her arms remained limp at her sides, and did not flail. The wail continued long and loud, what seemed forever to Savannah. Had she done the wrong thing? Had she misunderstood? Had she hurt the woman instead of helping her?

When the woman had exhausted all her breath in the scream, she flopped backward onto the bed once again, as if nothing had happened at all.

Savannah looked to the hallway, sure that nurses and doctors would be rushing in at any moment now. When no alarms went off, and no one appeared at the door after several moments, she slowly began rubbing the sap into the woman's stomach again. She remembered the wolf had thoroughly rubbed it into her own shoulder before, as she would a lotion, and it seemed the right thing to do. The woman did not seem to feel any more from her actions, remaining still and silent. The wolf made no move to stop her.

Savannah took the fact that no other person had been seen or come running in response to any noises or commotion to mean that she was indeed dreaming or hallucinating this. She was definitely still in her own hospital bed imagining all this craziness.

As the glowing sap dissolved completely into the woman's belly, the woman let out a long, slow sigh. Unless Savannah was imagining it as well, the corners of the woman's lips curved into the tiniest of smiles. Had she actually helped the woman? Had she eased the suffering of another? She felt her heart leap within her chest at the thought. Years of helplessly observing the suffering of others via the life of a journalist—whether for newspapers in the beginning, or on live television as she did now—had left her with a deluge of heartache that had nowhere to drain. It felt nearly ecstatic for her to help someone now, whether it was real or not!

The sight of the softly glowing tree reminded her she was only hallucinating.

But the elation felt too real to be all in her mind. All the emotions she had experienced here had felt so realistic. How could that be? She furrowed her brow, pondering these things.

"Well done," a rough, yet gentle voice said.

Savannah whipped around, eyes wide.

The wolf was looking directly at her, still sitting beside the woman on the bed. It opened its mouth for the first time she had ever seen, and said, "You were perfect."

Savannah turned and ran from the room.

• CHAPTER 6 •

WENDELL JOHNSON WAS UNAWARE he was being watched as he analyzed and compared the labels of every salad dressing on the shelf.

The one currently calling herself Sierra was never seen, if she did not want to be seen. She had had more years of practice at that than anyone could imagine—anyone still alive, that is.

She smiled as she simply stood in plain sight near him. She knew he couldn't help thoroughly comparing every label on every jar—he was an archivist to the core, obsessing over details nearly to the point of it being a case of Obsessive Compulsive Disorder, though he did not in fact suffer from OCD.

But he had been chosen for that very quirk.

It had not taken her nearly as long as she had expected to discover Johnson. She had been prepared to search for years for the right person, once she had determined she would need help for this, her latest and most promising task. If it had indeed taken years for her to find someone like Wendell Johnson, she would then have been low on time left for grooming that person to her purposes. The greatest risk she had feared in that was that in the meantime, the object of her purposes may have grown too strong or too distant to be of any use to her at all. Either extreme would have proven to have been too off balance.

But Johnson had practically come to *her*.

Up until thirty years ago, she had worried for centuries that the object of her efforts, the one she sought, the one she needed, would not be found, that she would not be granted another chance to redeem herself—and she told herself it *was* redemption she sought, not some petty revenge. She could rebuild all the Old Ways better than they had been before, and *prove* she was worthy. She was more sure of that now than ever before. All she had lacked was this one.

On the other side of that, she had also been afraid that the one *would* return, which had indeed happened, and so the fates had been on her side. Another chance had been presented to her, though not without new difficulties. Evolution always managed to play its tricks no matter what level it was at work upon. The important thing was that she had found him again, the one who had always been in her way, and then she had met and taken Wendell Johnson under her wing nearly immediately following, molding him into the perfect pawn she needed.

Now, these last few decades—a mere blink for her—she had not only been able to subtly shape the archivist without arousing his suspicions, she had also managed to manipulate circumstances around her object, her prey, and keep him in the suspended balance she needed until she was ready for him.

Yet Sierra was not so naïve as to expect it all to continue so smoothly. She held tightly to her caution and alertness; she did not allow herself to relax, though all her plans were perfectly in place in this present moment. She had learned *that* lesson permanently in what she had come to think of as The Beginning.

That time had caused her to become extremely careful—and extremely determined. Her personal vow to never repeat such a foolish blunder had instilled an endless patience in her that had given her the strength to survive the centuries. Her fear that all she worked toward would be for nothing once again held her mind on constant edge.

Fear was the first most powerful motivator for someone to accomplish a thing.

She had had no idea back then just how long she would be chasing her purposes. She had had even less of a clue she would live long enough to *see* it fulfilled.

But she had survived.

And she was intensely alert, though she admitted to herself just how much hope of success she also held close to her breast. That sort of attachment was a risky game to play.

She had continued to live as the centuries grew into millennia. She had found and adopted the perfect name for herself based on this: Sierra—a chain of mountains, jagged with peaks and valleys, and yet unbroken.

Sierra had naturally gathered an enormous amount of possessions over time, as well as a nearly unlimited sum of wealth scattered around the globe. These had enabled each of her schemes all the more freedom to be carried out as she pleased. There was nothing she was not able to arrange or accomplish.

These, combined with her awareness of what exists just below the surface of all things, made her power virtually unstoppable.

Or so she hoped.

She took pride in the fact she had not wasted the millennia merely searching for that one. Once she realized she *had* the time to construct such a thing, she had also had the wisdom and foresight to begin forming a vast and powerful network that she and she alone controlled, behind the scenes, as if the world were her own personal Oz, and she the great Witch behind the curtain. That little trick up her sleeve always made her feel strong. When she was in the security of her cemetery sanctuary, she felt even more untouchable.

The possessions she had collected and maintained were primarily books and documents of ancient, forgotten, and secret knowledge, many of which even archaeologists and anthropologists today would not be able to fathom. She laughed aloud each time she entertained herself thinking about revealing all she owned to some poor, unsuspecting soul. She imagined them comically keeling over from sheer delight and shock. Maybe she would try it one day, just to see if that would happen.

Sierra smoothed the cream-colored summer dress she wore as she moved silently down the aisle of the supermarket, keeping Johnson in sight as he made his way to the selection of freshly baked breads displayed to whet the shoppers' appetites.

She had hired Wendell Johnson under the guise of cataloging her collection, which she, of course, had no true need of either preserving or organizing. Her archives had not survived thousands of years by pure ignorant luck.

Exploiting his mental urge to specify details and apply organization, she had had no problems earning his utter devotion and loyalty. But she had not shown even him the full extent of her possessions. She had read every word in every document, and had found the old wisdom the ancient paths taught within them to be sound and true: The greatest control comes by *not* controlling.

Control of another is greatest when the one being controlled thinks it is all their own idea.

She had only shown and told him select information, though he had believed he was being entrusted with the whole of her estate. It had stroked his ego and his dreams, and made him extremely easy to deceive. He had been allowed to know only what he needed to know, so he would one day be in place to do what she needed, when she needed.

But now she was dead.

The time had come to begin the next phase of her plan, but Johnson had grown too comfortable with their relationship, and had nearly failed her. Or perhaps it was that *she* had grown too lax in her control of him. Sierra cringed at the thought of nearly repeating the Beginning mistake again.

Johnson had begun infusing too much of his own desires and projects into the work she gave him, splitting his time between his own research and what she told him to do, and sometimes disregarding her instructions altogether. He had done the former with the instructions she had given to contact and interview the Ferguson girl, taking too long to get it done, choosing to do so only after his own current study project had been completed. He had done the latter when she had given the most important instructions for setting this phase in motion. Sierra had then been forced to apply a level of emotional manipulation that could only have been done one way: leading him to believe she had died—and leading him to believe it was his fault.

Guilt was the second most powerful motivator.

Whether the guilt was groundless or authentic did not matter in the least; guilt always held a grip of steel, able to bind even the strongest will, if allowed a seat at the table.

Sierra had been furious when she returned from taking care of another piece of her plan to find he had not yet followed her instructions. In a rage that he may have destroyed thirty years of efforts, she had nearly taken his life from him, and in so doing had nearly caused the destruction of all her efforts herself, as well as the loss of most of her priceless, irreplaceable treasures.

The ancient texts were also correct in their warnings that anger does no harm whatsoever to your enemy, but instead sets only yourself on fire.

It never ceased to amaze her how even after so long a time, the most commonplace things still affected her. It was in moments like these that Sierra realized she was still human after all.

Johnson had never seen that side of her before. Sierra had always made every effort to appear as calm, generous, and compassionate as possible. She hated that other side herself, and attempted to avoid it at all costs.

But at the last second, as she glowered down into Wendell Johnson's panicked and horrified face, she had been able to pull herself back from the edge of that cliff, and spare his life, spare her collection, and spare her purposes. Once again, the knowledge she had absorbed from her hidden archives had provided her with the power to rein in the emotions that so easily overwhelm and shut down the rational, enlightened system, reminding her just how priceless her archives were.

And so she had killed herself instead.

In all the centuries she had lived, she had never faked her own death. The rare times she had stayed in one place long enough that it may have become necessary to change her identity among the community, she had always been lucky enough that everyone who truly knew her had simply died themselves. All she had had to do was seclude herself away for a time, and wait them out.

With the sub-surface skills she possessed, she had found faking her death to be even easier than she expected, though she knew she would never do such a thing again, no matter what was at stake. She had discovered it came far too close to yet another fear she hadn't quite been aware she held—the fear that she may legitimately die one day.

An extremely thin woman passing by caught Sierra's attention. Floral tattoo work was visible trailing down the woman's neck, and pieces of metal pierced the woman's face in multiple places. Sierra smiled as she drew a small jar of water from the sage green handbag at her side.

"Excuse me," she called to the woman as she removed the lid of the jar.

"Me?"

"Yes," Sierra replied, dipping her fingertips into the jar. "I wonder if I might ask you a question."

"All right," the woman answered.

Sierra removed her fingertips and suddenly flicked

them at the woman, spraying water droplets directly in her face.

"What the—"

Sierra's fingertips were back in the jar. She held the woman's furious gaze calmly, and inhaled deeply. The woman froze mid-reaction as Sierra sent a command for silence via the water elements. The droplets on the woman's face transmitted the new information they now held from their new connection with the woman's chemistry. The water in the jar the droplets had once been a part of, and still remained connected to at quantum levels, received the new information. Sierra absorbed and analyzed the information quickly, though the woman's instant response to her command of silence had already told her as much as she needed to know for this brief purpose: the woman's will was pliable. The rest of the woman's history did not matter to Sierra, but she scanned the details of it from sheer force of habit.

"Please quickly approach the man with a briefcase in his shopping basket. He will be wearing glasses at the end of his nose. Repeat this message exactly as follows: I have received word from the mountains beyond. She informs you she has found a new connection from her current view, and you must interview Savannah Marcus at South Grace Hospital immediately. You know what to do.

"Now be quick—he is presently in the bakery section of this store."

The woman's enraged facial expression had slowly relaxed until it held no discernable emotion at all. At Sierra's command, she turned and smoothly headed toward the baked goods. Sierra followed closely, enshrouding herself invisibly once again.

Johnson nearly dropped the loaf of baguette bread he was inspecting when the woman tapped him abruptly on the shoulder. Sierra smiled broadly, never tiring of the entertainment his nervousness had provided her year after year. His wide eyes and open mouth simply stared at the woman in surprise.

"I have received word from the mountains beyond," the woman began. Johnson managed to drop the bread to the floor now as his face paled in a heartbeat at her words. "She informs you she has found a new connection from her current view, and you must interview Savannah Marcus at South Grace Hospital immediately."

"What!" he exclaimed too loudly, interrupting as he looked wildly around. "How is this possible? Is she here?" He did not see Sierra standing nearby.

"You know what to do," the woman completed her message.

Johnson gripped her shoulders. "How did you get this message? How is this possible?"

The woman blinked.

The archivist's hands clamping her shoulders registered in her awareness, and instantly her temper returned.

"What the *fuck*, man! Piss off!" She roughly shoved free of his grip and began stomping away. Several customers paused around them to observe the commotion.

"Wait, please!"

"Creep!" she called over her shoulder.

Sierra nearly laughed aloud as Johnson stood immobile, as torn in deciding whether to chase the woman or continue shopping as he had been in deciding which salad dressing to purchase.

Sierra wasn't worried. She knew him well enough to know that he would do as she wanted. His sheet-white face alone was enough to tell her she had gotten his attention without him ever laying eyes on her.

And then Wendell Johnson surprised her.

He suddenly grabbed his briefcase from the shopping basket, shoved his glasses up his nose, and followed after the woman.

Astonished, Sierra trailed after him.

"Please! Tell me how you heard from her," he pleaded as he reached the woman.

The woman whirled around. "*What* is your problem, man? Quit harassing me! I got pepper spray, you know!"

"Please, how did she get the message to you?"

"Who?"

"Sierra," he replied, "The Mountains Beyond—that's how she used to sign off when contacting me while she was away from home."

The woman sized him up, a confused look crossing her features. "What is wrong with you? Are you sick, or just crazy?"

"I'm not crazy; I'm an archivist. But please—you just delivered a message to me. I need to know how."

"A message."

Johnson nodded.

"Man, I have *no* idea what you're talking about."

"Is there a problem here?" A security guard that had been alerted by other customers scowled at them both as he approached.

"Oh! No, I—"

"Yes," the woman spat out. "This man grabbed me, and keeps following me!"

"You grabbed her, Sir?"

"Well, yes, but—"

"And he's talking all crazy! Says I gave him a message."

"A message?"

"And I did no such thing! He's fucking crazy!"

"All right. Sir, I think I'm going to have to ask you to leave the store now."

"No, please!"

"Come with me." The guard grabbed his arm roughly and began pulling him toward the front of the store.

"But I need to speak with her! If she could get a message to you, perhaps you can get a message to her? Don't you understand—I need her! I'm lost without her now! She—"

"Move," the security guard commanded as he pulled

Johnson directly past Sierra. "Please continue your shopping, folks. We have everything under control here. I apologize for the disturbance."

Sierra stared in wonder as another security guard arrived, and the two guards ushered Johnson out the front door, still babbling about messages. Johnson had never shown such boldness and initiative in all the years he had been with her. He had always been the perfect and submissive assistant, never acting until being told to—where had he come up with the nerve to pursue the woman, much less abandon his carefully selected groceries after such agonizing choice making? Had he grown *that* attached to Sierra? *That* dependent? Was she still able to rely on him to carry out the plans she needed him to? Had her manipulation and attempts to control backfired on her?

Had her purposes been sabotaged at her own hand after all?

• CHAPTER 7 •

THE CART NEARLY TURNED over as she collided into it at full speed. She gasped as she threw herself backwards in an attempt to compensate the balance and save the cart. The man that had been pushing the cart down the hallway sprang into action as well, and both their efforts managed to stop the cart and rescue it from an overturned disaster.

Out of breath from her sudden flight from the wolf, Savannah looked up at the man. Dark brown eyes met her own. His mouth dropped open slightly as he stared at her.

Where had this man come from? There had just been no one in the hall—she had looked right before the wolf had spoken to her, and she would have heard the sounds of anyone coming down the hallway, especially the sound of utility cart wheels rolling across the linoleum.

The wolf had *spoken* to her.

It *talked*.

Why had that startled her? After all she had experienced with the wolf, why had that been what made her run away? She was all right merging with a neon tree with the wolf, but freaked out by the fact it could talk?

And why had she run from it? It was all only an hallucination in her mind, wasn't it? That couldn't hurt her.

Maybe that was the reason. Maybe her hallucination talking to her made her feel just that much crazier, as if she were talking to herself. She remembered a documentary on mental institutions she had seen as a young teenager. It had scared her on a certain level, and she had to admit she did have a fear that she may end up the same way one day. Still, she had hoped it wouldn't be until she was very old, if it happened at all.

Maybe the drugs they had her on were wearing off now, causing her mind to shift and begin perceiving the visions as an illogical threat, activating her fear, and rejecting the experience.

She broke her gaze with the man and looked back into the hospital room she had just run out of. Where it had been dimly and surreally lit only a moment before, the room was now fully lit, with patterns of sunlight shining through the blinds, and every fluorescent bulb glaring brightly from the ceiling. Savannah could see the woman in the bed lying as still as she had last seen her, and hear the continued monitoring and beeping of the machines she was plugged into.

And there was no wolf or tree in sight.

Savannah stared at the room, unable to wrap her mind around what was happening. The surge of adrenaline had to have caused the last of the drugs to wear off, allowing her mind to snap back to reality. The drugs could certainly explain the way she had seen the room in all its neon shades of pastel, but they did *not* explain how she got into that room.

"You're Savannah Marcus."

The bed curtain was pulled back, exactly how Savannah had done with her own hands, and the woman was without a doubt the same woman she had rubbed the glowing sap on. How were those facts explained? Her journalist's mind was caught in a whirlpool.

"Uh… Miss Marcus?"

She looked back to the man gripping the cart, then

quickly stepped back into the room. She had to see if the blue sap was still on the woman's stomach.

"Are you all right? Are you hurt?" the man asked as he followed her in.

Savannah reached the bed and stood still. The woman's gown was still raised, exposing her stomach. Both of the woman's hands were clutching her belly.

"Do you see the blue sap?" she asked without looking up, feeling the man come up beside her.

"Blue… sap? No…" he said slowly.

She turned and looked at him. He was tall, but being tall herself, they were off being eye to eye by only a few inches. Savannah found his eyes thoughtful and powerful, yet comforting and familiar somehow. He held her gaze unwaveringly as she searched their depths for any signs of mockery or disdain. She found none. Of course she wouldn't find anything—he had recognized her by sight, even in a frumpy hospital gown, and known her name, hadn't he? He was probably one of her thousands of fans around the city.

Well, her shattering of her perfect television personality image here by rambling about blue sap was also reason enough to cause a fan to begin looking at her differently, wasn't it?

But something about this man made her feel like she could trust him, as strange as that sounded.

"Yeah," she whispered, "Neither do I."

He continued to stand silently before her, unsure what to say or do. All the senses she had perfected early in her career interviewing people for the newspaper told her he held an honest sweetness and caring to him, though it was kept buried inside and protected.

Yes, she could trust this man.

"You aren't supposed to be here," he finally said.

She broke eye contact again to glance around the room. "Oh! I, uh…" she stammered, "Yeah. I really don't know where I am—I mean, I can see from your key badge that

I'm still in South Grace, but this isn't my room."

The man broke into a warm smile. "No," he said, "This is not your room, or at least the room you're supposed to be in. You're supposedly upstairs one flight, but I was just up there. You weren't there." His smile faded slightly. "And you weren't anywhere in the building, either."

"They're looking for me, aren't they?" she sighed. Sometimes she hated being a celebrity. Miraculously surviving an attempted assassination hadn't made her any less forgettable, she knew. She'd never be able to blend into the crowds again.

"No, I don't think they even realize you're gone yet."

She furrowed her brow again. "Then how did you know they can't find me anywhere in the building?"

The man studied the sleeping woman's monitors for a few seconds before replying, seeming to formulate his answer carefully. "I was the only one looking for you," he finally replied, cryptically.

"Ah," she smiled. So he was a fan.

Still, she picked up no danger from him. Her instincts confirmed to her again he was not a stalker or one of the crazies every person in the public eye inevitably gets. Or a disgruntled offender like the one who had tried to kill her.

"What's your name?" she asked.

"Audric," he replied as he smiled that warm and disarming smile of his. "Audric Kamen. Most call me Audi."

Savannah couldn't help smiling in return as he looked away almost shyly. This man was definitely a sweet one.

She looked to the ceiling suddenly, a thought occurring to her. "My room is one floor up, you said?"

"Yes."

"Exactly where on that floor was I?"

Audi thought for a moment, then chuckled. "Directly above this room, I think. Did you try to hide under your bed from the crowds, and fall through the floor?"

"If you only knew," Savannah answered, causing a look

of surprise from him at the seriousness of her answer. Maybe she wasn't losing her mind. Maybe she was, after all. She pinched the bridge of her nose and sighed. An urge to run and hide somewhere *was* quickly overtaking her. What was she going to do?

The buzz of the elevator in the hallway made them both turn. Savannah suddenly gripped his arm.

"You work here; you know this place," she said. "Can you help me? I'm really fine, as you can see, and I *really* do not want to be here anymore."

"Do you mean you want me to get you completely out of the hospital?"

She nodded emphatically, her eyes imploring. He seemed on the verge of protesting, but then footsteps from the hallway took the thought from his head.

Audi peeked around the doorframe of the room. He saw a solitary man carrying a briefcase heading the opposite way from where they were. He held Savannah's forearm gently but firmly and pulled her toward him. "This way," he said.

Leaving the supply cart behind, Audi led her from the room, and pushed her around the corner ahead of him. He turned to look at the man at the other end of the hallway again just before he slipped around the corner behind her.

"What is *he* doing here?" Audi frowned.

"You know who that was?"

He nodded slowly. "He showed up at my house yesterday, and knew things about me that no one knows. Things about my past."

"That's scary," she replied. Things about his past? Savannah wondered if she had been too quick to decide on the sweetness and safety of this man. Her journalist sense had never failed her before. "Did he see you just now?"

Audi shook his head as he ushered her on. "The stairwell is right up here.

"He had a lot of information on me, and I was not comfortable with that at all. I made him leave my house. I suppose it doesn't surprise me he came looking for me here, too."

"Or looking for me," Savannah said as they hurried along. Audi nodded thoughtfully. "Who did he say he was with?" she asked.

"He claimed he was only an independent archivist. Said Wendell Johnson was his name."

"Yeah, that all sounds legit," she said as she rolled her eyes. "And… this may be my ever-present reporter talking, but can I ask what sort of things from your past?"

"You're a reporter?"

She glanced sideways to see he was grinning. "Oh yes, I've even been on TV!"

Audi laughed out loud as he pushed open the door to the stairs and held it for her. "He had some old documents I was mentioned in."

"Ah, I see." She headed for the downward stairs.

"I didn't know they even existed," he added. "Wait, Miss Marcus, we're going up, not down."

"It's Savannah. And, up?"

She won another of his smiles she was quickly growing to love. "Like you said, *Savannah*, I know this place."

They emerged on the roof of South Grace Hospital, and crossed the helicopter landing pad. Audi used his passkey card to access another door.

"This medi-flight elevator will take us straight down to the emergency room, and thirty feet from the rear employee's entrance."

"What will they do when they do discover I'm missing?" she asked. "Will you be suspected or in trouble?"

"No, no one saw me with you, and I'm planning to keep it that way."

"And is it your habit to take strange women from the hospital home with you, Audric Kamen? You didn't hesitate a second in knowing how to sneak out of here unobserved."

Audi stopped and met her eyes. "No," he answered

seriously, "I never have before. I just… I keep to myself. I've watched and learned the routines of everything around me. I figured out how to avoid people. My own space is… important to me."

Savannah smiled and took his hand. "Then I am honored you would allow me in your space."

"Oh, you've been in my space before."

"I have?"

"Well," he said, "I have to confess I *have* seen you on television a time or two."

• CHAPTER 8 •

"GOOD EVENING, FRIENDS, I'M Cliff Perkins, filling in for Savannah Marcus, and this is your evening report. Thank you for joining me.

"As most of you are aware, our own Savannah Marcus was unexpectedly shot last night while beginning her nightly newscast. We want to let everyone know Savannah *is* alive and recovering remarkably well at this time. We at news channel seven sincerely apologize for the disturbing images our viewers witnessed before the cameras were able to be cut off air. It was certainly quite a shocking, unforeseen, and traumatic event.

"Tonight, we want to assure you the gunman *was* quickly apprehended. In quick-witted response, one of our own interns, Lance Barnett, gripped one of our studio cameras and shoved it into the gunman's head hard enough to stun the attacker, allowing our security team to detain and disarm the attacker. We would like to recognize and thank him publically for saving us all from further harm.

"The police have now released more information regarding these circumstances, including the testimony of the gunman.

"Carl Walcott, the attempted assassinator of John

Bridges as he ran for mayor, has spent these last four years in Stephens County Detention Center, largely due to the award-winning reports pieced together and broadcast to the public by Savannah Marcus, which led directly to his capture and arrest. Walcott fully blamed Savannah for his failure, and apparently continued to nurse the grudge in prison.

"Early yesterday morning, he became the third convict to mysteriously break out of Stephens County, and made his way directly for channel seven studios to attempt his revenge. How Walcott gained access to our building, much less acquired a gun in such short a time remains as unknown as how he managed to escape prison in the first place.

"But thanks to our local hero here, Lance Barnett, and the law enforcement department of Grenville, the would-be assassin has once again failed, and is again behind bars.

"Police have no comment at this time on the repeated success of inmates escaping from Stephens County Detention Center.

"And of course we all wish Savannah Marcus a continued speedy recovery, and look forward to her taking her rightful place at this desk again soon.

"Now, let's take a look at the forecast for—"

"Well, at least they told everyone you're still alive," Audi said, muting the television, "But didn't mention you were missing."

Savannah nodded. She had asked to watch channel seven's evening broadcast, to see what they said about her being shot. Audi sensed she wanted to watch it to make sure they did her show correctly as much as she wanted to find out what they said about her, but his arm hadn't needed much twisting to turn his old outdated nineteen-inch television on. He wanted to see the show as much as she did.

"They wouldn't broadcast that I was missing, even if they know yet," Savannah replied. "We know *someone* knows I'm gone already, but whether the news station knows yet or not I mean."

It was Audi's turn to nod as she continued. "At least now I know exactly what happened to me, too. They wouldn't tell me this morning when I woke up, only that I had been shot."

Audi watched her take another sip of the hot tea he had made her after they had eaten the light dinner of pasta and salad he had whipped up. He found it astonishing that Savannah Marcus was actually in his house, but he had never been one to be star-struck over celebrities and big names, so the afternoon and evening with her had been smooth and comfortable. He had been a bit surprised at how different she was off camera, how down-to-earth and *real* she was, though he knew he shouldn't have thought otherwise.

How she was *well enough* to be in his home right now was still a mystery to him.

"You're familiar with the hospital's procedures—how have they handled missing patients in the past?"

"I'm not aware it's ever happened before, except with the senile or delirious ones. They never manage to find their way off the floor, much less out of the building," he chuckled. "They get escorted back to bed without being reported to the local news channel."

Savannah smiled the smile millions of people had seen millions of times, yet Audi wondered how many had actually ever felt the warmth he now felt in this smile genuinely given to him in response to his little joke. He quickly averted his eyes, glancing back to the television to not seem as if he were staring at her.

"One," she said.

He looked back to her questioningly.

"One. I've only allowed one person to get close to me. That's what you were wondering, wasn't it?"

"How…"

She smiled broadly at him again, her blue eyes

sparkling. "You rescued me from being a needless prisoner without question or ulterior motive, and have spent the day alone with me, in your own home, respectfully never once trying to broach the topic of any of the questions burning in your mind." She turned facing him beside him on his sofa, tucked her feet up underneath her.

"And I feel very comfortable with you; I feel I trust you, so I want to confess something to you: I did not get to be such an excellent journalist by luck alone. Oh, part of it was a matter of being in the right place at the right time, but the majority of it was my sense of people." She furrowed her brow in thought. "More than a sense of people," she continued, "Like, I can sense that you won't hurt me, but I think anyone can sense regular things like that.

"What has made me a successful journalist is more than that—it's like I can *read* people. It's like I know what they're thinking, or know what they're about to do *before* they do it." She motioned a hand at Audi. "Like you were just wondering how many people had ever *truly* known me, right?"

Audi nodded, unsure how to respond. Savannah nodded in satisfaction.

"So," she said, "That confession should answer two of your questions at once—how I knew what you were thinking, and how many people I've let close to me."

"I…"

She held her hand up again. "I know, I can be very forward—it comes with the mentality, you know, but I also feel you are a very understanding and nonjudgmental man. I think you see and hear and know more around you than you let on."

"Yes," he smiled.

"And you're so sweetly shy!" she laughed, then added, "And… damaged, in some way…

"But I am very grateful to you for today, and don't want to make you uncomfortable or impose on you in any way. My life has been turned upside down in more ways than you know right now, and," Savannah glanced away then back to him, as if momentarily shy herself, "You were exactly what I needed. You gave me the space and time I needed to process and think about some things in safety. You were grounding for me, and I thank you."

"Well..." Audi trailed off.

"So ask me whatever you like. I'm ready."

Audi leaned back into the sofa. He hadn't been aware he had even leaned forward, and found himself grinning at her. "The interviewer is now the interviewed?"

"You got it," Savannah laughed, breaking further tension.

"Well," Audi began, "All right. The obvious first then: If you were shot last night, how are you perfectly fine now?"

She nodded, clearly expecting this question first.

"I'm going to trust you here. And you may throw me out on the street afterwards, but... I think I had a dream while I was unconscious. Or dead," she said, knitting her eyebrows again. "The nurse told me I had died."

"Wow," Audi said.

"Yeah... anyway, I had a dream, or a vision or something while I was out. In it, a huge white wolf came to me. It took some sap from a tree, and rubbed it on my shoulder—the same shoulder I had been shot in. Then I fell asleep in the dream, and—"

"When you woke up, you were in the hospital."

"Perfectly fine," Savannah nodded.

Audi waited silently. He remembered Savannah looking for "blue sap" on the patient's bed when they'd met. The pieces were coming together; he was content to wait for her to continue to reveal them in her own time. She was studying his face, probably probing him with her sensing as well, he guessed.

"You don't seem surprised, or confused, or skeptical at all."

"And you don't know my history," he replied smiling,

enjoying her bafflement. Savannah's mouth dropped open a bit, then closed.

"You said you *think* you had a dream," he said. "I'm guessing you say *think* because what happened in the dream turned out to be what happened in reality, too?"

"The being healed part, at least, yes," she answered. "That, and for one other reason: The way you found me. Or ran into me, rather."

"The way you weren't where you were supposed to be."

"Yes…" Savannah seemed to struggle for words to express her thoughts. "I *was* where I was supposed to be… and then I wasn't."

"You remember being in your room on the twenty-first floor?"

"If that's what floor it was, yes."

"But it was *you* who ran into *me*—on the twentieth floor. I was making my supply delivery rounds."

"I thought you said you were looking for me."

Audi laughed. "Well, I was. But not at the time you ran into me."

Savannah was confused, but let it pass. "Do you remember me saying you didn't know how true it was that I had fallen through the floor?" Audi nodded. "Well, I remember being in my room, but then I guess I fell asleep again. I woke up, and saw the tree again."

"The sap tree?"

"Oh, sorry—no, that was a different tree, but a tree is also how I got down to the wolf's world the first time, when it healed my shoulder." She rolled her eyes. "See? This sounds crazy. You're going to throw me out of here."

"No, really," Audi assured, "It's fine—please go on!"

Savannah sighed in frustration. "Okay. So I woke up, and the tree was at the end of my bed. I got up and touched it, then the wolf appeared again, and we went down the tree. We sort of slide down it, but it's not really sliding like you would down a pole.

"Anyway, we went down the tree into that lady's room, the room you said was directly below mine.

"Audi," she leaned close to him, "How did my *actual* body get down to that room if it was only a dream?"

"Wow…"

"And you saw me, and I'm here now, so I know it wasn't part of the dream—I nearly knocked your supply cart over running from the wolf!"

"You were running from the wolf? I thought—"

A sudden knock at the door was followed immediately by the tone of the doorbell. Audi and Savannah's eyes met instantly.

"You can hide in the coat closet here," Audi motioned as he passed a door, then peeked at the porch through the side window.

"It's that Wendell Johnson," he whispered to Savannah as she slipped into the closet. She nodded before pulling the door closed on herself.

Audi waited a few moments, then opened the front door.

"Ah, Mr. Kamen," Johnson smiled as wide as he could, "We meet again so soon!"

"When you know where I live, and come to my door, that's not so astounding," Audi replied simply. "Why are you here again, Mr. Johnson?"

His smile faded slightly as he glanced nervously to the side, then tried to peer around Audi's shoulder. "I, uh—"

"Are you looking for something?" Audi asked, making it clear he had no intentions of allowing him inside.

"Oh, no, I assure you—I've actually come hoping for your help." His index finger shoved his glasses up his nose.

"My help."

"Yes! You see, I know you work at South Grace Hospital, and, well, I mean I'm sure you already know that Savannah Marcus, that anchor on channel seven, is—or was—in your facility." Audi simply stared at him, a brick wall offering no confirmation either way. "Well, uh, I say *was* because, well, she's not anymore. I mean, she's supposed to be, but I had gone to see her earlier, and I overheard some of the staff. It seems she checked herself out somehow, except she did not check out.

"Would you happen to know anything about that, Mr. Kamen?"

"Why would it be assumed I know anything about that? Just as you know I work there, you also know I only stock the supply rooms and occasionally help clean up some of the nastier messes."

"Because, Mr. Kamen," Johnson smiled another smile that seemed not-so-nice this time, "I also overheard that 'Audi' had uncharacteristically left his rounds incomplete, and they had found his full supply cart still in the hallway of floor twenty."

Audi's heart skipped a beat as he tried to maintain his masked appearance. All afternoon, he hadn't even thought about leaving his cart behind, or leaving work. He was used to working on his own, coming for his shift, and going when he was done without reporting to anyone. The other staff was used to him keeping to himself—it hadn't even occurred to him that his leaving might be noticed. Had they associated his disappearance with Savannah's? Did they think her disappearance was foul play, and suspected he had something to do with it? The hospital had taken the extra security precautions, so it could make sense they'd think it was foul play, but surely the hospital staff knew him well enough that they wouldn't suspect him as being capable of such a thing?

On the other hand, wasn't that old saying 'It's always the quiet ones you have to watch?' He should have at least rolled his cart into the supply room of that floor before they left.

Maybe he was more star-struck with Savannah than he realized.

"Yes," he said, "I wasn't feeling too well earlier."

"Ah," Johnson said, "It must have been quite a sudden

illness, to ah, abandon your cart so suddenly. I hope you're feeling better now?"

"I am."

"Good, good. Then you, ah, don't know anything about Savannah Marcus?"

"No, I don't."

"Then I suppose you can't help me after all. I was hoping you at least knew some inside information about her 'miraculous' recovery," Johnson leaned closer, looking Audi directly in the eye, "Or about the woman whose room your cart was found just outside of."

"Woman?"

"Mrs. Rhonda Garner, late-stage stomach cancer," Johnson twirled the air with his fingers, "Cured."

"Cured?"

"Overnight. Another miracle! And in the same hospital as Savannah Marcus."

Audi had no clue how to respond.

"May I come in, Mr. Kamen?"

"No, I'm busy."

Johnson looked past Audi into the house again. "I see.

"Mr. Kamen, I, ah, I'm sure you recall the newspaper copy I showed you yesterday."

Audi's stare began to turn into a glare.

"And you remember I mentioned I'd had a visit with your beautiful friend Rachel?"

"Just *what* are you insinuating, Mr. Johnson?"

"I know what you can do, Audric. I've read many accounts of others like you, and I don't believe it is mere coincidence that not one, but *two* miracles have happened around you in the last twenty-four hours."

• CHAPTER 9 •

————————◄ ►————————

THE DARKNESS NO LONGER bothered him. It had become so familiar to him, so comfortable, he rarely remembered anything else, or noticed that anything was other than it should be.

And the waiting; he no longer realized he was waiting.

How long had it been? Centuries? Or had he only been confined in this darkness a day or two? It didn't matter.

Time had lost all meaning and measure for him. But then again, they had meant very little to him even before this moment, hadn't they?

He really didn't mind, either way. He was still here, and *that* was what mattered. As long as he was here, as long as he was able to think, he would be able to wait. No one knew where he was anyway. He had been afraid for a few weeks or decades at first that someone was left, that someone would find him, that his end would come after all. But no one ever came. No one ever found him. And so he had begun to relax at some point of the way.

And one day, maybe next week, maybe today—what difference did those words mean to him?—he would be able to move again; he only had to remember *how* to move. When that day came that he was able to move once again, he would be able to *do* things again, and he definitely had things to do. He had already decided on that long ago, or just a minute ago.

Perhaps time would be important to him again then, too. He could imagine needing to work within a concept of time again—hadn't he done it before? He couldn't quite remember. That may have been only a dream. Regardless, he would do what he needed to do; he had seen it from his place outside of time.

He had also seen all that had happened before. He had seen it all over and over again. That was what kept him alive in this deep, silent void. Or was it the nutrients he had discovered he could absorb from the soil encasing him that kept him going? He had figured that out yesterday, or last year. No, it was definitely the memory of the things he had been through before that fueled his desire to keep waiting.

And he had done this himself, hadn't he?

The tiniest drop of dew dripped from what slight space there was over him, and landed on his head. He felt it. He allowed the thoughts of what happened before to slip from his mind as he smiled at the dewdrop. He could pull in as many nutrients from the earth he wanted, but it was a rare occasion to find and draw in actual moisture. He savored it as if it was giving him an entirely new body.

He still had a body, didn't he?

He focused on the molecules of the dew as it soaked into his scalp, merging and becoming a part of him. Yes, he definitely still had a body. He forgot sometimes.

His thoughts landed back on what was to come.

When he moved again, they would all see him. They would all see who he was. They would all see what he could do. He would be the one they came to for their every need. They would quickly realize that in their hard times, he would be their shining wayshower, and that in their easy times, he would be their vigilant watchman. They would appoint him to a high place, and he would be—no, all that was what he had already been before, not what he would be to come, wasn't it? Or was it?

He couldn't quite remember sometimes.

How long had it been?

A drop of water fell on his head.

Excitement shot through his system. He definitely still had a body—he was positive about that now. He wouldn't have been able to feel its outline, its shape, as the surge of adrenaline coursed through it otherwise. *Before* did not matter. What was to come did not matter. This moment had brought him not only the infrequent taste of dew, but now, too, a larger drop of water to be thoroughly enjoyed!

Perhaps he did not need to be expending so much energy on such intangible things as *before* and *next*, and instead concentrate his efforts into finding more of this irresistible, satisfying *moisture*. Oh, how he had forgotten! How long had it been? He hadn't felt this since he was out and around, *before*, and all had come to him with their every need regarding the sun and stars or earth and sea, and all—No, no, that was *before* again. What mattered was what was coming up. The things he would be able to show them was what mattered, and this water on his head.

No—only the water on his head mattered right now, didn't it? Two drops in one day—imagine! This *was* still the same day, wasn't it? Maybe that was last week he had felt the dew. Did it even matter? He decided it didn't. It was a miracle, and the miracle was all that mattered. All else could—

Another drop, even bigger!

If his vocal chords had been used in ages, he would have been able to cry out in joy as the sensation from the molecules soaked into his scalp and interacted with his own cells.

Three drops in a single day! He truly was blessed; surely this was a sign he would accomplish all he had set his heart to, and once he moved again, all he touched would be gold in the eyes of the stars! When the time to move again came, he would—

Two more near-simultaneous drops landed on his head, and his ecstasy froze in a heartbeat, then rapidly melted to fear.

Oh no. Please, no.

Four more drops, one after the other, paved the way for the steady trickle of water that followed. Each new drop-within-drop increased his anxiety and confirmed his fears.

Her.

He felt it.

He read it.

He received the message in the water loud and clear.

Suddenly, he was no longer buried in the earth.

He turned and drew back the dark, heavy drapes that had held the sunlight from his sanctuary for so long. He had done this *before*, hadn't he? Or was this *now*? No, this was *before*. He had resolved that these draperies never be pulled open again, and he should have simply had the window sealed up with stones or even precious metals, for inspiration, but had not. He had been too focused on his work, too committed.

Now the audible sounds of the crowds below his window blended and blurred with the impending messages he had been ineffectively attempting to ignore and desperately searching to conquer, and he knew he had lost. He had run out of time. All he had fought for, all he had waited for, all he had been promised was now being murdered, stolen, ripped from him with no opportunity to defend, much less attack.

And it was all *her* doing.

He whirled around as the massive wooden doors to his area burst open. The armored soldiers of the Seeker's camp poured in, nothing but their eyes exposed. His own eyes frantically ran over his possessions, panicked, seeking what could be grabbed before *he* was grabbed.

They were on him before anything was able to be rescued, dragging him swiftly to the door. He felt the vibration of his voice making sounds he had never heard before as he screamed in protest. He glimpsed his tools and his work engulfing in flames as he twisted and fought— work he had devoted his every waking moment to, work he had nearly perfected, work that would make him even more indispensible to the Ancient and the people, if he was only given a chance to prove it.

The sight of fire being set to all he owned pushed him immediately to his breaking point.

Nothing was left to lose, if these were lost. Nothing would be gained if he didn't try, and he had to try; he had not worked so diligently on this magic and ability for nothing—what better test was there than the very real situation of these soldiers dragging him from his own sanctuary? He could show them all right; he could show them all, right here.

Abruptly, he ceased his struggling and closed his eyes. He allowed the sounds to continue rising from his throat, and brought his full awareness to the vibration they created. Then he shifted a portion of his awareness to the vibration of the floor boards as they shook beneath the stomping of the soldiers' feet.

Mentally grasping each end of this vibrational rope— his voice on one end, the solid wood of the other—he inhaled sharply, drawing each vibration to the center of his belly, then exhaled as hard and fast as he could, willing the vibrations to enhance in strength tenfold as he shot the vibrations down his arms and out his hands, which were being firmly held apart by the soldiers.

The thunderous blast that impacted the soldiers on each end of his arms sent them crashing into the soldiers behind them. He immediately dropped to the floor in the confusion, and threw himself out the door. Shouts and yells filled the air of his previously peaceful sanctuary, adding to the rising cries of the crowds in the streets below. The soldiers scrambled to their feet and toward the door after him as he leaped to his feet and spun to make his escape—and suddenly stopped short.

She was standing there, still as an idol, an image of perfect calmness amidst the uncharacteristic chaos that had escaladed within the city these past months—chaos that had now peaked in this chain of events here and now. It was her doing, all of it. He knew it. Everyone knew it.

And she was right here.

She had won.

The soldiers took hold of him again, careful to grip only his forearms this time rather than his hands, all while she merely stood watching it all, as if it were the most commonplace thing in the world.

Never speaking a word, she gracefully turned and began to walk away. The soldiers dragged him behind her, following.

His shockwave had worked, and would have worked, would have spared him this predicament, and quite possibly his life, had she not been there. And this was not the first time she had gotten in his way, was it? She was the entire reason he had secluded himself away in efforts to speed his progress and preparation. But his labors were not for his own soul, as she thought—this is how he knew that *he* was the one in the right. He had done his work for the benefit of the Ancient, and though the Ancient did not yet know, he would see.

Or would have seen.

She led them all into the underground chambers that tunneled beneath the city. As they passed beneath the main streets, the rumbling and ruckus of the crowds above could be heard and felt even this far below ground. Dust and pieces of the stone supports broke loose and dropped among them periodically.

Sudden inspiration struck him.

Perhaps there was still a chance.

Wasting no time debating internally, he zeroed his focus in on the sounds and vibrations the warring crowds above were creating, inhaled the vibrations into his belly center, amplified its strength, and shot it downward, into the earth, adding the sound of his own voice to the power again as well.

He was amazed how much easier this level of magic was the second time, and marveled as the crater below him yawned open before anyone realized what had happened.

The soldiers cried out, releasing his arms as they twisted and desperately grabbed at the edge of the hole to save themselves, while he willingly surrendered to tumbling directly into the center of it.

Even at this turn of events, he had still heard no sound or utterance from her as he pulled vibrations from anything and everything his awareness could touch, and blasted himself diagonally deeper into the earth, deeper and deeper each time, finding it easier and easier with each thrust until he felt he was a safe distance from her, from the city, from everything.

Now nobody knew where he was.

No one would be able to find him, and he could simply wait here a few weeks until all the disturbance and uproar worked themselves out, leaving his city, his home, in peace once again. He would rebuild his sanctuary, and begin his work where he had left off—this time with the renewed faith and confidence from his experience escaping *her*.

But she *had* found him now, hadn't she?

It had been more than a week, hadn't it?

The walls of his temporary earthen sanctuary suddenly seemed to close in on him, darkness flooding his awareness even faster than the trickle of water dripping on his head was soaking his hair. He had been so clever, so careful— hadn't he? Where had he gone wrong?

The water dribbled down his face, and he felt a tingling numbness slowly spreading through his body. As the water reached his shoulders and began wetting his chest, he felt his body completely paralyzed—or more accurately, no longer under his own control.

She had him.

Remembering that his mind was clearest, and his

chances of finding and attempting an escape were greatest when he was calm and submissive, he willed his mind to resist struggling to make his body move. Panic would only make things worse.

Ramika, he thought upwards, knowing she would be able to hear him through the water connection she held on him.

I am no longer called that, came the instant reply. *I have become Sierra.*

Tears immediately welled below the surface of his face, but were denied the gift of birth. His mind reeled and tried all the more desperately to take control of his body and his weeping.

So it was true.

He *had* lost track of time. He had waited too long to return to the city, to his work. He had allowed *her* too much time to hunt him down.

And now she had him again.

How did you find me?

I always knew where you were, Prophet. I found you the same day you buried yourself within this self-appointed grave. I simply didn't need you yet.

Levels of dread never felt before shocked his nervous system.

She had known, all this time.

He had never been safe, never been hidden.

How long has it been?

Time is measured differently now as well—not that time ever held any meaning for a prophet, hmm? But in the way we counted it in the Old Days, it has been over two hundred and sixty thousand cycles.

How was this possible? How could she be speaking truth? Yet that was what she had always done, wasn't it? That was her service in the city.

What do you want with me, if all is… lost?

The same thing I wanted with you before.

But if all is now gone… Are we the only survivors?

We were. We are no longer. I thought I had things firmly in my control and would not have need for you, but I am now concerned that is not the case.

Then it seems you are still repeating your own patterns, Ramika.

Call me Sierra! I am no longer that other—she foolishly grew too comfortable, too arrogant to succeed. I am new. I—

Have just confessed you've done the same once again: relaxed in a false confidence as your prize slipped from your hands.

No! I have not! I am here to retrieve you to ensure I do not fail again—this shows I am not the same!

He made a silent mental note regarding the weakness and sensitivity he had discovered in her, for future use, as he relented, to watch and wait.

How could I possibly be of any help to you, if it truly is a new world? I know nothing of it.

Silence followed as Sierra seemingly debated whether to continue

Suddenly he became aware of a low, rumbling vibration slowly descending around him on all sides. It grew in intensity until it was deafening to his trained senses, even after all this time.

What are you doing?

Mental images immediately flooded his mind. Rain. Trillions of endless drops of rain, crashing onto countless people, metal moving objects, oddly shaped castles, endless tree and plant leaves, and hosts of all sorts of animals. He felt each and every drop on each and every object—individually, and as a whole simultaneously. Visuals of all the energy, all the information, all the sound being gathered into a massive vortex high in the sky and slammed down directly over his earthen sanctuary overwhelmed and overloaded his system.

Just as suddenly, all but the rumbling around his body disappeared.

Precious vibrations for you, Murphy, she stabbed into his mind. *Get up here* now.

• CHAPTER 10 •

"**H**E IS NOT THE one who healed me," Savannah interrupted as she came up behind Audi and pulled the door open wider. The exasperated look Audi gave her as he stepped aside did not faze her as she continued. "Rather, the staff at South Grace is absolutely exceptional, and clearly performs their duties at top rate standards, wouldn't you say?"

"Miss Marcus! Mr. Kamen was just telling me he knew nothing about you, yet here you are in his own home."

"I asked Mr. Kamen to help me. He was only trying to honor my wishes as he saw best," Savannah answered. "I think you need to come inside, Mr. Johnson."

"You ah, know who I am?" Johnson asked as he stepped into the house and looked around as if expecting to find even more people lurking. Audi motioned awkwardly toward the sofa, clearly at a loss as to what Savannah was doing. She was supposed to have stayed in the coat closet until he got rid of Johnson.

"A good journalist makes it her business to know as much about the environment she finds herself in as she can," Savannah said as she sat in the armchair opposite Johnson and crossed her legs—all business, Audi noted, amazed at how smoothly she was able to switch gears from how she'd behaved with him all day. "And so, now that you know where I am, as well as what's happened to me, I'm afraid I'm going to need some answers from you."

Johnson attempted an unconvincing smile. "Oh ah, well, yes, of course."

Audi fought smiling as Johnson nervously took the same seat on the sofa he had sat in before, clearly unprepared for the intimidation he was receiving from Savannah. Turning the tables was one of the trademark qualities she held that had made her such an excellent journalist. Many powerful people had surely been relieved when Savannah had stepped down from the hard-hitting expository journalism to simply run the desk of the evening news, though everyone had been taken by surprise with that seemingly backwards career move. As far as he knew, she had still offered no explanation for her decision to the public.

Audi was also realizing that Johnson was much more talk than action; he would nervously back down when the pressure he tried to apply was reversed.

"Why are you harassing Mr. Kamen?"

Johnson's jaw dropped. "Harassing?" He cleared his throat. "I'm not—"

"You have inserted yourself unsolicited at his private residence twice, and his place of employment once. He has his full rights to privacy, which you are clearly violating."

"Now wait a minute—"

Savannah held up her hand. "Further, you are now seeking to infringe upon *my* life and private matters, which I'm sure you do *not* want to do, as I have considerably more influence in this city than Mr. Kamen does.

"Now, I'm told you are 'simply an archivist.' But your words and actions are not confirming this proclamation." She leaned toward him. "Who *are* you, Mr. Johnson?"

"I am!" Johnson protested. "I'm only an archivist! I've specialized in organizing private collections for thirty-three years!"

"Collections, or collection?" Savannah pressed, continuing to show him she already knew more than he thought.

"Both, I assure you!" He shifted in his seat as he lost even more of his assertive act. "It's true that I've worked nearly exclusively with one collection in particular, but ah, I have done—and do—work with other libraries as well."

"Then why are you investigating *people*, if books are your business?"

"Well… I ah," Johnson stumbled. "You see, it's a bit of a long story."

"Well, since you are not leaving this house until you satisfy our questions and convince us we can trust you, it seems we have plenty of time to listen to a long story."

"Not leaving… You can't do that!"

"You chose to come uninvited and press yourself upon Mr. Kamen, so it seems we can."

"No! I was made to—it wasn't my idea! Believe me," he groaned, "I'd truly rather be secluded behind closed doors, tracing trails of history and knowledge through dusty documents!" Audi was astonished that Johnson seemed to be on the verge of tears. What was going on with this man?

"Who made you do it?"

"My friend," he answered quickly. "Though more like my employer I suppose."

"Why do they care about a simple hospital employee?—no offense," she directed to Audi.

Audi let a laugh out at that. "No, no, go ahead."

"Well…" said Johnson.

"And the truth. I'm trained to be able to tell a runaround when I hear one," Savannah said.

Johnson visibly swallowed and shoved his glasses up his nose. "Of course. I ah, I wouldn't dream of lying to you, Miss Marcus."

"I'm listening."

"Well, you see, my friend ah—she warned me to never

reveal her name to anyone, no matter what happens, you see—approached me nearly thirty years ago now. I was a young and excitable boy really; fresh out of college and feeling I could change the world. I had just begun my private archivist business, insistent I didn't need to work *for* anyone to do what I loved. I turned out to be right when only a few years into my ah, efforts—and growing quite desperate, of course; had nearly decided to begin applying for employment at larger agencies—Miss ah, I mean, my friend approached me with an offer that seemed too good to be true."

"Which was…" Savannah prodded.

"Oh, that any and all of my own personal projects would be funded with no questions asked if I would agree to devote the majority of my time to her—ah, to their services."

"We already know it's a woman, Mr. Johnson," Savannah said. "You told Mr. Kamen as much on your first visit."

"Did I? Oh. All right, yes. Her services." He glanced around the room again uneasily.

"And what exactly was it about you in particular that brought you to her attention?"

"Oh, well, you see, I do have a side project, or a hobby really, that I enjoy on the side of my work. I ah, I have always had an interest in what can be classified as paranormal subjects—the science discovered behind them, specifically. At one time—at the time she approached me, actually—I maintained a newsletter of selected data regarding such paranormal reports. This was a good ten, twelve years before the internet was in full effect, but somehow she knew of my publication, and said she chose me specifically for her needs, based merely on my hobby work!" he declared proudly.

"So this collection of hers contains a lot of 'paranormal' material?"

"Oh yes," he grinned, his face lighting up, "And much,

much more!

"I was in pure heaven! My ship had come in, and I had it made. Now here I am, thirty years later—who knew?"

"So would you say her main interest is in paranormal activity?"

"Oh no, not at all. Well, yes, much of it is, but I've helped her organize so much else over the years that I don't think I would say that, no."

"And she is who sent you to speak with Mr. Kamen."

Johnson nodded.

"Was her interest in Mr. Kamen paranormal?"

"Oh yes," he replied excitedly, then seemed to think better of it. "I mean, ah, well… She seemed to indicate that ah, well, he is ah… very important to her. Well, she took great interest in him."

Savannah and Audi exchanged glances.

"Would you say the documents you brought to Mr. Kamen's attention capture your friend's interest in him?" Audi knew he had not told her exactly what the newspaper had been about, and had not told her about the photographs Johnson had shown him at all. He found himself very impressed with her abilities of intuitive interrogation—appearing to know facts she did not fully know in truth.

"They were the beginning foundation of it, yes," Johnson nodded. "She hadn't really told me *all* she had in mind, you see, but she ah, I do know she had hoped to establish a… relationship with him."

"A relationship."

"Oh, dear me—not a *romantic* relationship," he chuckled, seemingly embarrassed, as if he were an adolescent school boy who had just heard someone say the word *sex*. "A *working* relationship. She wanted to personally know more about what he could do. She considered the evidence on record to be too distant, too far removed—as I can surely relate to in my studies of ancient customs and what have you—but she always stressed that it was curiosity only; she would never have hurt him—you," he aimed at Audi, seeming to have forgotten he was actually present, "I assure you."

"So why send you?" Savannah asked. "Why did she not simply approach him herself?"

"Oh ah," he cleared his throat, "She was an extremely intelligent woman; seemed to possess a much older soul than her appearance indicated—but isn't that true of so many people these days, with all the surgeries and technology available?" he nodded, agreeing with himself. "But she thoroughly understood the human mind, and claimed people were always much more willing to assist her if they were coerced more... subtly?"

"Manipulated, you mean," Audi suggested, speaking for the first time. "Deceived."

"Oh no! Not at all!" Johnson protested. "It's only that people are much more ah, excited to do something if they feel it was *their* idea."

Savannah looked to Audi, handing control to him.

"I see," Audi said, "Thus the mysterious pointing out of the phone number on the back of your business card."

Johnson suddenly sat up straighter. "I refuse to answer anything else until *my* questions are answered, too," the archivist declared, his simulated boldness returning. "That was the deal."

"I don't recall making a deal," Savannah said.

"But—"

"I told you to come inside and answer my questions," she snapped. Johnson's act wilted once more.

"I don't know any more," he practically whined.

Audi nearly wilted himself as Savannah's gorgeous blue eyes caught and held his. A dawning shot through his system as he realized that seeing her in action, so closely—and in *his* defense—was causing him to admire her all the more. The way she took all the vague hints of his most confusing and hidden past in stride, as if they were the most common things in the world, made him marvel all the more. Of course, she had risked her *own* self in trusting him with *her* dream or vision or whatever had happened to her. In a way, the two were similar, weren't they? Even as he thought on these things, he knew he would soon be opening more of his story to her as well.

Savannah raised her eyebrows at him, questioning if he had more to say. Audi shook his head. She broke the eye contact, and turned back to Wendell Johnson.

"So this woman was dead *before* you approached Mr. Kamen?"

If Johnson had seemed distressed before, he grew visibly distraught now. "Yes!" he cried out louder than Audi expected, startling him. "Oh God! She was—is!" The man buried his face in his hands, eyeglasses and all.

Savannah looked at Audi, clearly not expecting this reaction herself. Was she feeling bad about it? Audi's time he had spent with her today had given him a sense of how different she really was from her "work personality," and now led him to believe the expression on her face meant she was sorry for pressing Johnson so hard.

"Uh," she began, "Mr. Johnson?"

Sobs racked his body all the more. Audi and Savannah waited in silence.

"I did it," Johnson finally wailed. He lifted his face, his breaths coming in short gasps. "I did it!"

"You... killed her?" Savannah asked cautiously.

"I didn't mean to, but I did it! I did!"

Audi watched Savannah shift in her own chair, and knew she was seriously beginning to regret launching into this now; she had clearly gotten more than she bargained for. Were they hearing an actual confession of murder here? What would they do about it? What could they do? Surely Savannah would know, with her experience in the field of such things.

"Mr. Johnson," Savannah crossed her legs again. "How did you kill your employer? Are you telling us you murdered her?"

"No! I mean yes—but it was an accident, I swear on my

own mother who gave me life!

"You see," he continued, eyes darting around the room, "She also loved another of my pastimes—my cooking. Well, she claimed to love it, anyway; I've actually seen her eat only a handful of times in all my years with her, if you can believe that," Johnson attempted a chuckle that quickly drowned in his upset nerves, "But every so often, she would not only allow me to cook for her, but *invite* me to do so, in her own kitchen.

"The night she died was one such occasion. You see, though she provided me with a residence of my own, it was still separate from her living space—separate buildings entirely. There were often great stretches of time I never saw her at all, even when she was at home, in town.

"She had been away for quite some time," he paused and cleared his throat, "Well ah, she had always left to travel periodically—to search out new treasures for her collection, you know—but her trips away had grown increasingly longer and longer. I'm a bit ashamed to admit I first began to notice because I found my own projects advancing more quickly than usual; she hadn't been leaving me as much work to do—neither in person, nor by note or message from abroad, as was common for her." He seemed to relax a bit as his mind wandered deeper in thought. Audi snuck a peek at Savannah to find her expression a bit more comfortable as she listened patiently to Johnson.

"Well, she had been away for one of the longest periods I seem to remember, and ah, I *had* received a couple messages from her during that time of leave. I had been ah, engrossed in researching some extremely fascinating theories on how ancient wonders had been accomplished, such as Egypt's pyramids and Easter Island's moai monuments, and well… I'm afraid I allowed the time to slip by without accomplishing her requested tasks in a timely manner." Johnson heaved a long sigh.

"She returned unexpectedly that day, literally startling me as she actually entered my area to collect the details of the tasks I had unfortunately not yet completed. I hadn't even known she was back home," he whined.

"After working with someone for thirty years, you feel you know them pretty well—and even feel connected to them at times, which is not far from the truth at all, when you get down to the quantum levels of things, which is another utterly fascinating subject, I might add," he pushed his glasses up his nose and sat a bit straighter, even more relaxed by his own rambling distraction. "Well ah, in all that time of working with her—for her—I had never seen her react the way she took the news that I had not done what she asked." The archivist wilted once again at the memories in his mind, the corners of his mouth turning down, instantly adding at least a decade to his appearance. "She ah," he fumbled, "She… did not take it so well.

"She had always, always been so kind to me—gentle, even—and certainly more generous than anyone's wildest dreams could have imagined.

"But when I told her I hadn't spoken to—ah, well, done what she had asked of me," he wiped at beads of sweat that had formed on his forehead, "A look of such… Such…"

"Mr. Johnson?" Savannah said softly as the man broke into tears again. "Are you all right?" What had happened that would reduce such a seemingly intelligent and logical man to such a weepy and emotional mess?

Johnson managed to nod as he inhaled deeply and removed his eyeglasses completely to rub them on his jacket sleeve. "It's just ah, I've never seen that sort of look on anyone, much less someone I considered a true friend. I honestly don't know what caused such a response from her. Surely I had been a bit slow or delayed in other tasks she had set me to over the years? But I always got them done, and she never complained once about my work in *all* these years!

"But that look…" A shudder visibly shot through his body. Replacing his glasses, he slowly raised his eyes to meet Savannah's.

"I tell you, Miss Marcus: I literally feared for my life in that moment. She suddenly seemed something wild, something... possessed? Tearing at things, shoving things over—nearly *roaring* in pure... rage!"

"How did you escape?"

"I didn't," he whimpered. "I... I had been knocked to the floor, lying among precious books with their spines cracked open too wide, their pages dog-eared and creased, priceless documents and scrolls ripped and bent." He lifted his hands and looked at them quickly. "My hands had landed in the liquid preservative from the jars of very rare sea specimens that had been on the shelves, now smashed. The fluid stung and burned my skin...

"I was on the floor, unable to move, unable to get away... She was over me, looming over me *so* close—and the look on her face! The look!" he sobbed. "Oh, God! I was *so* frightened, so unexpectedly *horrified*—I thought my life was about to end!

"And then she just stopped."

Audi and Savannah's eyes met. Audi released a breath he hadn't realized he was even holding.

"She stopped!" Johnson shouted in a sort of exhausted joy.

"And then what did she do?" Savannah asked.

Johnson sank back on the sofa, exhaling. "She left. Without a word, just turned and left.

"I was quite bewildered, as you can imagine. I don't know how long I simply laid there, bruised and burning, terrified she would come back in. I had no clue if something had happened to her during her trip that I simply happened to trigger, or *what* had just occurred.

"Eventually, just as I had decided to begin trying to clean up the mess she had left in her wake, she called me from the main house, inviting me to come use her luxury kitchen and make a dinner for us. She said we clearly needed to talk.

"You can imagine my wariness after what had just

happened, but ah, I also felt the pressure of having to comply, having to do what she said, for fear of another outburst—it was such a shock to me that she would behave like that, you understand. I truly did not know what to make of it," he said, shaking his head sadly.

"So I left the mess the way it was, and went to see what she had in her pantries and refrigerators that I could turn into a dinner. I knew I was in trouble for not doing my task; was I about to be sacked? Let go? Any perspective and predictability I had for her had been instantly shattered, and I had no idea what I was walking into.

"I had selected a chicken and was preparing a special mixture of about a dozen different herbs to apply to it when she came into the kitchen to see what I had begun." Johnson smiled faintly. "I was greatly relieved to see she seemed pleased with my choice. I was even happier when she leaned in and smelled the herbs I had applied to the chicken, then smiled and said she had had some fresh asparagus delivered from a nearby farmer that would go excellent with the seasons I was preparing."

Johnson paused thoughtfully. "I ah," he cleared his throat, "Come to think of it, I did find it a bit strange at the time that fresh produce had been delivered while she had been out of town so long, but I was such a tangle of nerves I hadn't allowed the thought to fully form… But, that doesn't matter now at all," he sighed.

"I had put the last touch on the chicken, and started it in the oven—all as she stood by watching me. I felt like a fly in some sort of spider web—plagued with fear and the feeling of impending doom, but helpless to move away or do anything about it.

"I then went to the back of the kitchen to look for the asparagus in the pantry—which is really an entire room to itself, you see—and when I returned, I found the kitchen nearly engulfed in flames!

"I dropped the clusters of asparagus, and made my way to the fire extinguisher, beating at the flames with my apron to get to it. As I began spraying the fire, I noticed something large in flames on the floor in front of the stove. To my horror, I realized it was *her*—and she wasn't moving!

"I desperately put the rest of the fire out and rushed to her," he buried his face in his hands, "But it was too late! I killed her! I still don't understand what happened. I must have done something wrong with the oven—I should have checked it better before going to get the vegetables!" He broke into sobs once again, drawing out the word *vegetables* as his body shuddered.

After a moment, Savannah cleared her throat. "Mr. Johnson?"

"Yes, yes," he struggled, "I'm fine, I'm sorry."

"No, it's all right. I... I'm sorry you experienced that," she offered, convinced by his story and emotions. She glanced to Audi before continuing.

"I am curious, though, Mr. Johnson: You say your employer has passed away, yet you are continuing the work she set for you? Surely she had business partners, or at least family to inherit the collection?"

"No ah, like I said, Miss Marcus," he sniffled, "She wasn't exactly my employer, and ah... well, I haven't told anyone but you."

"You did not report the death?" Savannah exclaimed, leaning forward in surprise.

"Well ah, no..."

"Mr. Johnson!"

"Wait, wait!" he cried, waving his hands back and forth. "It's not like that—no! She left orders not to! Just as she made me swear to never reveal her name, no matter what, she also made me swear that if anything ever happened to her—anything at all—that I was to not inform anyone anywhere, if I could at all help it." The archivist groaned and pressed his palm to his forehead. "Who knew that that 'something' happening would be at my own hand?"

"So you simply did nothing," Savannah stated.

"I ah, disposed of her... body."

"How did you do that?" Savannah asked after an unsettling pause.

"I incinerated her in the kiln of her pottery house—the pottery house she has on the property, though I also never saw her or anyone make use of it in all my time there..."

"And she left orders to continue her work, if she were to die, or did you come to that decision yourself?"

"Oh, she left plenty instructions—both verbal and written. I always thought it was odd, as if she expected something to happen at any moment. Oh, I ah, also have all the necessary documents naming myself as legal owner of all her estate, should the need ever arise."

Savannah cocked an eyebrow. "How did you come by those?"

"My friend was adept at making sure all her bases were covered. She had wills officially drawn up for every scenario she could think of."

"Was she paranoid?"

"I'd rather prefer the word thorough."

Audi was completely speechless as he sat looking back and forth between Johnson and Savannah. It was clear Savannah fully believed the man's story, and he had to admit he found himself believing it as well. An insight suddenly occurred to him.

"I was the 'task' you hadn't completed yet, wasn't I?" Audi blurted out.

Johnson sat motionless on the sofa, not fidgeting for once.

"No," he finally replied. "Well, in part, but no, it wasn't you."

Audi suddenly knew. His heart leaped into his throat before slamming immediately back to his stomach. He had known this was coming, hadn't he? This had been his nagging dread the last twenty-four hours, hadn't it? But no, he had thought, surely he wouldn't see this man again;

surely he could avoid him, avoid this—if he came knocking again, he simply wouldn't answer the door. But catching sight of Johnson in the hospital had nailed the dread home just a bit further, hadn't it? And the knock on the door this evening had been another hit. He had known who it was. The insistent chime of the doorbell had sealed the deal.

"Rachel…" he whispered.

Johnson looked to Savannah quickly before shifting back to Audi and nodding slightly.

Audi could feel Savannah staring at him. He knew she didn't know about this, but this man very clearly did. He felt as if he were burning up, and knew his face must be flushed red.

Suddenly, Savannah reached over and placed her hand on Audi's leg. He looked over to meet her eyes, and instantly saw the message in the unexpectedly intimate gesture: *I don't know what this is about, but it doesn't have to be pressed right now.*

"Why am I now in this picture?" she asked, steering the archivist from Audi. "Why were you looking for me? I've only just met Mr. Kamen this morning."

Johnson instantly paled.

"Mr. Johnson?"

Johnson's eyes darted to Savannah suddenly, wide and frightened. "I…" he stammered, "I ah… don't know."

"Did she tell you to talk to me, as well?" He nodded, trembling. "At the same time she asked you to contact Mr. Kamen and—" she caught herself, thinking better of it. "The same time as the others?"

Johnson slowly shook his head. "This afternoon…" he replied in a low voice.

"She told you to contact me this afternoon? But I thought you said she was dead."

"Yes, she is…" the man murmured as he fell sideways, unconscious.

• CHAPTER 11 •

———————◄ ⟩►———————

AUDI DID NOT WANT to be calling the number on the back of the business card. He didn't want anything to do with any of this; what he wanted was his normal, peaceful, routine life—no more, no less, though the addition of Savannah Marcus in his life *would* be a welcome change he'd like to keep, he had to admit.

When Johnson had fainted on his sofa, Audi and Savannah had discussed what to do with him. Savannah was not ready for anyone to know where she was yet, and though they both believed Johnson's story, the fact he had so much private information about them left a distrust regarding him. Audi had suggested calling the police and having them lock Johnson up, but Savannah had been hesitant that he would tell the police where she was.

Why the man had passed out in the first place had baffled both of them—and his comment on having heard from his employer that day, while still confirming she had previously died was even more confusing to them. His apparent unstableness alone was enough to want to be rid of him.

"But we still don't know why he was looking for *me*," Savannah had pondered. "You and I have never met before today... have we?"

Audi had confirmed that they had never met, although the already familiar closeness that had been between them since sneaking out of the hospital together had made the answer feel odd somehow. Their eyes had remained locked on each other's in silence for a few long moments. Audi had resisted the sudden urge to grab her and hug her—or more—as his mind had raced to say something else.

"As crazy as it sounds, how bad would it be to tie him up here somehow, so we can get him to talk more later, while keeping him from talking to others yet? How big of trouble would we be in?" he had laughed self-consciously.

"I was just considering the same thing."

"You were?"

Savannah had nodded. "I think we could easily pull the 'harassing intruder, self-defense' card, if it came down to it," she had wrinkled her brow then, "But I don't think he will actually be any trouble for us, even when we let him go, if we play our cards right. He seems to be incredibly loyal to—and scared of—his employer, and of all this he's gotten himself wrapped up in. He's not going to want anyone else poking around too much. The big question is what *does* he want with each of us? Or what does his *employer* want, rather."

"I think you should have been a lawyer instead of a journalist!"

"Me?"

Audi had nodded. "You handled that entire interrogation like you were in a courtroom or something. Very professional and cold."

"Cold!" she had exclaimed in mock horror before they both had broken into an easy laughter.

"Let's risk it. What do you have to tie him with?"

"I should have known you'd say that, actually," Audi had replied. "You do have a habit of throwing away chances to advance your career, don't you?"

"What do you mean?"

A moment of dread had shot through Audi's system. He had only meant to joke around with her—had he offended her now? Gone too far?

"I only meant how you stepped down from roving reporter to read news from a desk. I'm sorry, I didn't mean to offend you; I was only trying to be funny. I just had in mind how everyone made such a big deal about you going backwards in your career... Sorry... I shouldn't have."

"Oh, that," she had replied. "It's all right."

They had wrestled the still-unconscious Johnson into Audi's spare bedroom, and secured him to a sturdy dining chair with a length of tan-colored twine Audi had retrieved, and then had tied the chair through the hinges of a closet door.

As they stood inspecting their handiwork, Audi had said, "You know, at the front door, he said he was looking for you because of your miraculous recovery."

"And he seemed to think you had something to do with it," Savannah had instantly replied.

Audi had let out a nervous laugh at that. "The amazing reporter caught that, did she?"

"She did," she had said, flashing him the smile that lit up her blue eyes again.

"So... she wants to know why."

Savannah had shaken her head. "Not unless you're ready. You are my safe zone at the moment, and I'm not about to press my luck and risk pushing that away. I feel very comfortable with you, and am not ready to leave or be pushed out the door quite yet."

"But I just tied up a man hostage in my home—isn't that the sort of thing your job requires you to notify authorities about?"

"You did? I didn't see anything."

"Oh. Then," Audi had looked away, then back to her, bashfully, "I'd like to wait a bit on that story, if it's all right. I mean, not because I don't want to tell you, or because I'm hiding anything—I think I'm still just trying to sort it out myself, you know? It's something that hasn't come up in a very long time, and I'm not sure how it's making me feel quite yet."

Savannah had held up her hand and smiled, and then had leaned in and kissed his cheek softly.

"Then let's begin our own investigation now."

"Now?"

"No time like the present!"

"Aren't we waiting for Johnson to wake up?"

"We are," she had replied, "But didn't you mention there was a phone number you were supposed to call?"

Now the line at the other end of the number that had been handwritten on the back of Johnson's business card was ringing, Audi's cell on speakerphone so Savannah could easily listen in. Audi felt anxious and stiff from the combination of Savannah's closeness and the unknown he was stepping into with this phone call. Having a man tied up in his house didn't help matters much, either.

When Savannah placed her hand on his arm, perhaps sensing his anxiety, his full awareness was on that touch until a voice at the other end sent a jolt through him.

"Hello?" the voice answered.

Audi's peripheral vision instantly began to dim. The pounding of his heart in his chest reminded him he needed to breathe, and as he consciously inhaled another breath, the mist cleared a fraction.

"Hello? Who is this?" the voice asked.

He knew the voice, and it was the last voice he had expected to hear, though when looking back later, he knew he probably should have suspected it. But he had assumed this was the number for Wendell Johnson's boss, and had further assumed and expected no one would answer, since it was known she was dead.

How was *this* the voice the phone number belonged to?

"Who *is* this?" the voice insisted.

"Um," Audi managed to mumble before he felt himself falling to his hands and knees, landing over the body of a young woman lying on the floor. The heavy, gasping breath of the woman blew across his face as he leaned close.

"No," he whispered. "No, no, no, no!"

The woman opened her eyes slightly, their bright hazel color flashing as they met his own eyes before closing again as she turned away in a violent fit of spasms.

"Rachel!" Audi cried out.

A small movement caught his attention at the corner of his eye. He turned and saw a woman standing nearby. "Savannah?" That wasn't right. Savannah hadn't been here. Nobody had been here this day—how *he* was even here again, Audi did not know.

Spasms and retching turned his attention from these thoughts and back to Rachel on the floor. "No, no," he whimpered, "Not again, I can't do this! I'm not ready, remember!"

"Puh…" Rachel struggled. "Please…"

With a sob, Audi wasted no more time. He reached out his left hand, and placed it on Rachel's forehead, and then placed his right hand on her upper arm. With eyes closed, he inhaled as deep as he could and threw back his head. Two more spasms shot through Rachel's body before she grew still on the carpet before him.

Audi's breathing had increased to a deep and rapid rhythm. His head remained toward the ceiling, eyes closed, and his hands trembled slightly. In his mind, he was grasping the corners of the room, drawing it in, pulling its atmosphere down into his palms, and then shoving it out his palms to Rachel's body.

Over and over, he repeated this internal movement, each round gaining an intensity and desperation as his own breath grew slower and slower.

A final, soft moan escaped Rachel's lips before her body went completely limp. Audi removed his hands from her, and lowered his head.

"Rachel?" He gently gripped her chin, turning her head toward him. "Rachel!"

No movement or response from her sent Audi into motion. He dashed to a phone on the wall, and hurriedly punched three numbers on it, whispering "No, no, no…"

The old phone in his hand was suddenly his modern mobile phone again, the screen displaying the call duration of the last call, now disconnected. Audi stared at it in confusion and disbelief for a moment before whipping his head over to where Rachel had just been lying. The floor was the living room of his own home again, and empty of any bodies.

Savannah removed her hand from Audi's arm. The change in pressure caused him to glance at her before turning back toward the floor, his mouth slightly open in disorientation.

"Audi," she began, "I… I saw that."

He looked fully at Savannah, speechless.

"What was it?" she asked. "*Who* was it?" When Audi was unable to answer, she added, "Someone you cared very much for, I could tell."

Audi nodded sadly as he sank to the sofa.

"It's part of the story you're not telling yet, isn't it?"

He nodded again as she sat beside him, and placed her hand on his leg.

"You were stretching out dozens of tentacle-like arms, grabbing chunks of thin air, and pulling them down to the girl," Savannah said after a few minutes of silence. "When you grasped each piece of invisible air, it turned bright glowing blue, just like the trees I've been seeing in my dreams or visions, or whatever they are."

"You saw all that?" Audi asked. Savannah nodded. "I wasn't even aware of it, but… that could describe almost perfectly what I do—what I *used* to do—with that."

"You were trying to heal her."

"And failed," Audi added. "How did you even see that? How were you there? I saw you standing there."

"I think because I was touching you," Savannah mused. "Maybe the direct contact transferred the experience to me as well, or took me along with you, whatever happened." She let out a sigh that blew her dark bangs from her forehead. "God, if someone had even mentioned things like this to me even last week, I would have thought they were off their medication. But now," she collapsed backwards into the sofa cushions, but left her hand on his leg, "Given my own direct experience with my dreams slash not-dreams lately, I'm already not surprised by this, and, in fact," she sat back up and turned to face Audi directly, "This may even be connected to why we were drawn together, if you believe that sort of thing."

"Do you?" Audi asked, feeling more present again, whether it was the intimate and comforting touch of her hand resting on him, or if it was the initial shock of reliving the experience again beginning to fade. He *had* experienced the same sort of thing when Johnson had shown him the newspaper clipping from when he was a child, after all.

"Do I?"

"Believe in that sort of thing?"

Savannah smiled. "Yeah," she answered. "I guess I always have, secretly, deep inside this cold reporter's heart of mine."

Audi cracked a smile himself.

"So… that girl on the floor was who answered the phone, I gather, and that triggered the flashback."

Audi made a noise. "That's some flashback, if that's what those are—they're *very* realistic."

"They? You've experienced this before?"

"Yesterday, when Johnson showed me the old newspaper."

"Yesterday," Savannah repeated. "Do you remember that ever happening before in your life?"

Audi shook his head.

"Hmm. And yesterday was when I had my first experience—well, was shot, and recovered, with the help of blue glowing light, like you had in your hands just now."

"Do you think—"

A muffled scream suddenly interrupted.
Wendell Johnson was awake.

• CHAPTER 12 •

━━━━━━━◦( )◦━━━━━━━

WHEN THE RAIN HAD begun pelting the front glass covering of the moving machine again, they had made a sudden detour from their original destination—or rather, Ramika had. Murphy was merely along for the ride.

Thinking the rain storm she had used to get him out of his earthen sanctuary had finished for a while, she had said she was taking him to her castle—most of which was underground, she had informed him.

And that was all right by Murphy.

He would be perfectly comfortable with that.

Instead, they had now entered a graveyard, and gone to the back of the grounds, where Ramika—Sierra—had quickly begun stripping her clothing off, one piece at a time.

He watched in unashamed fascination, aware of the stirrings within his body that told him his masculinity was still fully functional, despite the identity of the woman he was watching undress. This *was* the same woman who had destroyed his home, his work, and his land, ripping away all he had known and believed. This was the same woman who had now returned to complete her capture of him, for her own purposes.

Yet when her breasts were exposed before him and began to shimmer in the wetness of the downpour, his felt his body betray his mind inside the strange robe she had handed him upon his resurrection from the earth, his own clothes having eroded away only the stars know how long ago.

When was the last time he had been with a woman? It was before he had entered full devotion to the Ancient, he knew that. Yet the mind and body never forget such things, and the memories of feeling a woman squirm beneath him, flesh on flesh, her moistness escalating from a warmth to a heat around him deep inside her until the world momentarily disappears in a flash of ecstasy for both souls overtook his senses as Sierra shed the last of her clothing and leaped to the top of a small stone shrine. The sight he witnessed between her legs as she spread them for stability and stretched out her arms caused all breath to leave his lungs in a rush.

No.

New name or not, this is still Ramika, the same Seeker who sought to tear apart all that was right and all that was just in the land—a land he had given all to defend, in honor of the Ancient. This was not just any woman, and certainly not a woman to mate with, especially not from of a mere lack of sexual contact. He had far better control over himself than to allow himself to relent to such desires. He was a Prophet, wasn't he? A true Prophet—not a false Speaker as this woman before him, however arousing her body may be.

Murphy willfully turned his back on the naked woman atop the mausoleum just as she tilted her head to the skies, giving herself fully to reading the rain that drenched her, and shifted his own focus to the water falling on him. She seemed completely oblivious to his presence, neither embarrassed by her actions being witnessed, nor concerned that he might now escape while she was in trance. He supposed she would be able to track him back down easily enough, if he did run. It would be a wasted effort to even try, he decided.

The pure water soaking his own body *was* divine, after so many millennia in the dry earth. He absorbed the energy of the moisture in an entirely different way than he knew Sierra was absorbing it. He felt the pure life of it fill and replenish the cells of his body, so long deprived. The strength returning to his limbs felt incredible.

Murphy took a peek over his shoulder. Sierra had not moved a muscle, and was still thoroughly engrossed in her reading. Feeling stronger, he closed his eyes, and swept his awareness over the clapping sound waves of the downpour, scooping up the vibrations, and shooting it forward before him, as physical feeling as any solid stone would have been. The vibrational stone cracked a carved ornament off the top of a tombstone in the distance.

Murphy smiled.

The magic still felt as easy and natural as it had been the day he had used it to escape his fate back in his old sanctuary.

Should he use it to try to kill Sierra now, while she was incapacitated as it were? He could easily knock her from the top of the shrine, and be on her before she had a chance to defend herself—if she weren't keeping a sliver of awareness on him, that is, which was entirely possible. She may have even seen his little test.

No. It was best to wait.

He would know the right moment when he saw it, and then he would strike, at last bringing an end to what had been started in another lifetime.

He sat in the grass where he was, his back still to Sierra, not minding the cold sogginess one bit.

What exactly were her plans? What had she been arranging in place? How had she survived all this time? How was she able to keep the same body in tact, much less her mind? As a Prophet, he had been able to keep his mind whole by skipping and traveling throughout time itself, maintaining a thread of sanity, but how had she managed to keep a steady mind watching hundreds of thousands of cycles come and go before her constantly? The wonder of it amazed him nearly as much as the perfection of her body excited him.

The wonders of this new world alone excited him just as much. The moving machine they had used to get here was a marvelous invention! What else did this magical world now hold? Perhaps what he knew of magic was considered commonplace and unimpressive here. Either way, he would learn it all, and find his place here, as he had in the days of the Ancient.

A sudden thought struck him. She had said they were the only two left from that time. That meant the Ancient was gone as well—difficult to imagine, but not impossible to happen.

So she had won in the end, it seemed.

The thought of both these facts ignited a fire of sadness deep within his belly that even the drenching rain could not put out.

Perhaps he should run, and attempt his escape. Even if she caught him again, he would have had a chance to learn more about this world on his own, without her influence or control. It may even give him a greater chance to defend himself and *not* be recaptured. He had escaped once before, hadn't he? At least until this day, he had.

Yes. He would try.

As quickly as he could, Murphy leaped to his feet, and was slammed to the ground again immediately. Bruises on his shoulders began to throb even before he realized what had happened.

Blinking the rain from his eyes, he found himself looking up at Sierra standing over him.

"Of course I was listening to you," she said calmly. "Try that again, and more than your shoulders will feel pain."

Apparently confident her message had been received,

Sierra simply turned and began redressing herself, somehow managing to wriggle her wet body into wet clothing.

Murphy's body no longer overrode his mind as he watched. All desire he had felt had completely died with the abrupt reminder of just who she was and what she was capable of.

The old anger and hatred had won.

CHAPTER 13

SHE ABSENTLY WATCHED THE wolf circling the tree. A remote part of her was aware she held the wolf's attention, that the powerful animal was watching her and her alone, but the rest of her—the majority of her—was lost deep in thought, not truly registering that the wolf held *her* attention as well.

Having donned a chartreuse floral headscarf and large Audrey Hepburn sunglasses, Savannah had disguised herself for going in public. She had laughed in the mirror at how silly she looked, but her desire to not be recognized had overridden all concerns about her personal appearance. She realized she had found her escape, and intended to hold on to it.

She had had a long, sleepless night in Audi Kamen's bed, thanks to Wendell Johnson's angry shouts from the other bedroom, where he and the chair he had been strapped to had remained tied to the closet door. Johnson's anger had slowly abated into a quieter whimpering throughout the night, and Savannah had even heard him fully weeping at one point.

How Audi had managed to get any sleep on the sofa was beyond her understanding. Maybe she was simply more sensitive to the distress of others. In fact, she knew she was.

Audi had seemed to recover fully from the unexpected contact with the girl named Rachel from his past, though he had remained quieter than before, entangled in whatever inner turmoil he held around that subject. He hadn't shared any more of that story with Savannah, but she felt he had shared enough for her to grasp the major emotions behind what had happened. In a way, it felt similar to her own inner complications—an overwhelming pull toward action, but a crippling feeling of inefficiency to accomplish that action.

It must be a man thing to be able to sleep soundly amid screaming prisoners and emotional disarray both, she thought.

Though Audi and Savannah had both expressed uneasy feelings about continuing to hold someone against their will, they had decided it was best to leave Johnson tied up for now, and for Audi to maintain the appearance of his regular routine and report for his shift at work. They were gambling everything on Johnson's fear of his employer—a fear that seemed to be firmly in place whether his employer was dead or alive—and their mutual feeling that what was happening to them was connected, important, and must not be stopped or manipulated, as Johnson seemed to be trying to do. Exactly what was going on, though, neither Savannah nor Audi could find the words for, and Wendell Johnson eerily had more facts about things past and present than they were comfortable with.

It was clear they had entered a whole new world, and their lives were changed from this point on.

Savannah had decided to try to gain some perspective at the city zoo, which had always been an escape for her whenever she felt too overwhelmed by the world around her—particularly by the pressures and emotions her job exposed her to. It had been even more overwhelming when she had had to work in the midst of the dramas that broke her heart. Choosing to take a demotion and merely read the news from a desk had provided her a bit of shielding, as she had hoped—a layer of separation between herself and the events—but she had quickly found that even that was not entirely enough. What more she could do about it, though, she hadn't known, and so had continued to suffer the barrage, as it was.

She had always loved and seemed to understand animals, and as a child, had thought she might become a veterinarian. Tasting popularity and success in school debating exercises as well as in organizing and reporting for the school newspaper had shifted her focus from animals, and Savannah had followed the seemingly logical course of doing what she was good at.

That was how the world worked after all, wasn't it?

That was how you survived.

But Savannah had not been surviving, and not a soul knew her true feelings and internal struggles—not even her sister.

The zoo had become a very special place for her, but she had never paid much attention to the wolves before, though it was no mystery to her why she found herself transfixed at the wolf pit today.

Her mind wandered to thoughts of what things would now be like if she had died from the gunshot wound in her shoulder. She would have been completely free from it all for sure, wouldn't she have? Never again would she have had to wrestle her own heart. There would have been no more cramming pain and sorrow down inside her so that she could present the world with a beautiful, calm, and collected face—or need to hide from the world inside a scarf and shades.

Release had been *that* close.

With the same skill she had developed over years of public communication, she quickly snuffed that line of thought from her mind, refusing to allow herself to go down that road again.

She had not only survived, she had experienced inexplicable things that had been very much real to her.

Had she died after all, and what she had seen was what awaited everyone on the other side? Was she *still* dead and merely dreaming all this? Was Audi a figment of her imagination? He *did* seem too wonderful to be true.

But she hadn't died again in the hospital room, yet had seen the tree and wolf then, too—unless it was *because* she was dead that she had seen it, and imagined it had teleported her entire physical body to another floor.

A sudden jolt shook her to the present moment as a small boy shoved his way between Savannah and the overlook rail, spilling orange soda down her leg as he tried to see the wolves inside the pit.

Well, I'm definitely not dead, Savannah thought as she inspected her wet and sticky pants. *I don't think I would have dreamed this.* The boy's horrified mother apologized profusely as she began dragging the boy away.

"It's all right," Savannah smiled.

A movement and a flash of light in Savannah's peripheral vision caught her eye. Her heart skipped a beat as she turned to look into the wolf pit. The wolf that had been slowly circling the tree in the center of the pit had sat down at the side of the tree, and a second, shimmering wolf was now circling the tree instead. Both wolves were looking directly at Savannah.

When it was clear Savannah's full attention was being received, the ghostly wolf stopped circling the tree and faced it for a moment before slowly pressing a huge front paw to the trunk of the tree.

It removed its paw, and sat on the side of the tree opposite the solid wolf. It began staring at her again, waiting for her to do something.

Savannah pulled the oversized sunglasses to the tip of her nose and looked over the rim of them. The wolf and the glowing paw print were still there, and the blue light from the paw print was visibly spreading to cover the entire tree.

"I can't get down there!" she exclaimed aloud before realizing a man with a toddler sitting on his shoulders was standing right next to her. The look the man gave her made her laugh and flush in embarrassment.

Knowing she couldn't look any crazier, Savannah asked, "How many wolves are by that tree down there?"

The man looked into the pit, then back to Savannah. "Um... One," he replied. "Are you all right? Is there someone I can call for you?"

Savannah laughed aloud again at that. "No, I'm fine. Thank you," she said as she turned to move to the side viewing rail of the pit, where less people were.

She rounded the corner and came to an abrupt halt. She was not on the continued pathway of the zoo trails, but at the edge of an overlook much higher than the wolf pit. As she stepped forward and looked down, she found no wolf pit beneath her, as well as no glowing tree or vision wolf. Below her was a massive crowd, spread as far as the eye could see. She gasped as her mind registered the thousands upon thousands of people below. Her hands flew to her mouth as she realized what they were doing.

Though she heard no sound, as if the volume on a television had been muted, she saw every single person in the crowd fighting and battling all who were around them. There seemed to be no sides taken in the brawl; everyone appeared to be against everyone else—each one for himself.

The flashes of red as more and more blood was shed in the slashing and punching filled her with a horror greater than she had ever seen abroad reporting for the news. Even those who had already fallen motionless to the ground were not immune, and were stomped on, kicked and stabbed repeatedly. The lack of sound lent an even more disturbing eeriness to the scene, as Savannah was impacted by wave upon wave of the sense of pure fear and terror rising from the crowd, nearly causing her to double over in physical pain herself.

The brutality she was witnessing formed instant sobs in

her throat. The sobs cracked into full shrieks as her eyes fell on a group of men and women holding down other men and women to be raped in turn by others in the group, even as they themselves were gashed and cut down. Savannah's screams echoed alone in the absence of any other sound, and she was startled as a man stepped up beside her.

Expecting it to be the father and toddler again, she turned to ask if he could deny seeing *that* horror below, but stopped short, catching her breath.

It was not the man from before, but Audi who stood beside her now. As he looked down to the mob, his face twisted into such an unmasked expression of sadness it seemed he would cry out himself any moment.

She started toward him, but then stopped herself.

Something was different. This *was* Audi, she was sure of it, and yet it was not Audi.

Looking him up and down, the first thing she took note of were his clothes. The deep, rich tones of maroon and brown were not what she knew of Audi's style, and the flowing, robe-like cut of his outfit was like nothing that existed today at all. His hair was longer, cut differently, and held more gray than she remembered. A lengthy beard also now grew from his jaw line. With all the physical differences, Savannah had no clue how she had even first thought this was Audi, but peering at his face and eyes confirmed to her this was indeed Audi beside her.

Looking down at herself, she found that she, too, wore a flowing style of clothing, though hers was white, and accented with a flowing half-skirt of a sheer maroon matching Audi's maroon over the lightweight, full-length gown.

What was going on here?

Savannah took a step backward again and looked all around for any sign of the wolf, sure it had something to do with this. The wolf had been present for, and was apparently the facilitator of, her previous unexplained experiences, but she saw no sign of it now—only the fact it had been in the physical wolf pit just before she found herself in this place.

Audi turned to look at her, definite tears in his eyes catching the afternoon sunlight and sparking at her. He held her gaze as he motioned weakly toward the crowd. His face twisted into full sobs as he was unable to formulate words. His hand dropped to his side again just before he dropped to his knees. Savannah rushed to his side in time to break his continued fall to the stone floor, the motions of it all strangely familiar.

"It wasn't right," he moaned as he rolled to his back, eyes squeezed tight. "It wasn't the right way, was it?"

"I…" Savannah said.

"No! No, my dear, you played your part—you played your part extremely well," Audi continued, peering through his tears. "You saw, and you warned; No blame rests on you. You are cleared, dear Lady." He struggled to sit up, then collapsed back to the stones. "It was I and I alone who chose this way—yet even now, my heart tells me it *was* the right way…" He covered his face completely with his hands as Savannah simply stared, speechless. "But look at them—LOOK at them! Why has it happened anyway? Why has all now been lost? How was *this* the 'right' way?"

"Do not speak these things until it is known for sure!" Savannah said, surprising herself. Where had that come from? It was as if the words to say had been in her mind, and she had merely repeated them. "Who can say what the One sees? Not even you."

Audi cried all the harder at this, reaching one hand to cup her face. "Ah, my dear Vena'atra, always the voice of reason, to the end. I honor you for your devotion." Audi inhaled a deep long breath and rolled his eyes to the skies. "But it is done, and you must go. They have chosen," he sighed heavily. "They have chosen, and now walk their own path. They have chosen the lies Ramika has spread over the tried and tested clarity I—and you at my side—have offered.

"There is no more we can do.

"Go now, before she comes. She is on her way even now."

"But you are this present ruler!" Savannah cried, her voice still echoing in the deathly silence. "Is there nothing that can be done?"

Audi shook his head as his body shuddered with a new wave of tears.

"Again you speak the truth, dear Vena'atra, even when it is unknown to even you. 'This present' is the key, and it is now ending. Look," he choked out, "Look to the people. Stand and look. You will know."

Savannah slowly stood and turned toward the crowd again, tears freely streaming down her own face. She did not know what was going on here, but the raw emotion of it had overloaded her system, leaving her fully immersed in the moment.

The dreadfulness of the crowds below shocked her system again as more people filled the spaces of those cut down as quickly as they fell. Her hands were at her mouth as she fought the screams from deep in her belly. What caused this? What did Audi mean he hadn't done the right thing? Did he honestly think he *caused* this alarming mob?

The images blurred and cracked as her mind raced. She had seen the blue tree and shining wolf right before this—she had been transported to another dream-like world, hadn't she? This wasn't real. She was not really seeing this. These things were not really happening.

Was this Audi's dream, a story his mind had wrapped around some guilt or self-blame that he held inside—maybe something about the Rachel girl? The thought of this being true made her cry even harder.

A sudden deafening roar assaulted her. The shouts and howls of the people reached her ears, the invisible barrier had been abruptly shattered, and she collapsed beside Audi on the stones, gasping for air.

"Go," he panted. "The Prophet has escaped. There *is*

still hope after all. Hide yourself, so the hope may be that much more. You know the Way—Go!"

"But what of you!"

"There is no space here now, the—"

"Do not speak these words!" Savannah clutched his clothing and buried her face in them.

"The time has come. My cycle is done."

Savannah screamed in a panic.

"Ma'am? Hello, ma'am? Are you all right?"

She looked up suddenly. Her headscarf and sunglasses lay beside her. Her body was stretched across the pavement, and her legs were partially in a muddy puddle yet to evaporate after last night's rain. She noticed the brown of the mud mixing with the orange soda already soaked into her pants, creating a nearly black stain she thought vaguely resembled the shape of South America. Savannah's thoughts wandered to the time she had been to South America to record video segments from the site of Mayan pyramids for a documentary her station had hired her out to narrate. She had been taping the final scene when a massive storm—

"Savannah Marcus?"

Her mind snapped to the present and it was then that she realized the overwhelming roar of the crowd below had fallen silent. She quickly propped herself up higher to look into the wolf pit of the zoo once again—a pit with only one, solid wolf inside.

That was the last thing Savannah remembered.

• CHAPTER 14 •

▬◗ ◯ ◖▬

AUDRIC KAMEN FOUND A small group of coworkers clustered near his locker when he arrived. Their instant silence and the tension hovering in the room left the chatter of the weekday morning television show the only sound in the lounge, revealing they had indeed been waiting for him to arrive.

"What's going on, guys?" Audi asked, breaking the spell after a moment of awkward staring between sides.

Charles, who had been set to guard Savannah's room the day before, stepped forward and waved Audi closer. "Aud, man," he whispered, looking around nervously, "What are you doing here? I mean, it's good you came, you know—proves your innocence and all, but…" Charles trailed off, glancing around again, appearing extremely worried.

"My innocence?" Audi asked. "What are you talking about?" He looked back to the group behind Charles to find each of them hanging intently on every word.

"They didn't even try to call you? Oh man…" Charles wrung his fingers and leaned toward the doorway for another peek. "That is cold, man, *real* cold. They're just gonna show up and drop it on you."

"Drop what? Charles, what is going on?"

Charles leaned even closer. "You know Savannah Marcus disappeared yesterday, man?" he asked softly.

Audi fought the urge to swallow, knowing that that would be a sure sign of guilt to all the eyes on him in that moment. "The reporter you were guarding yesterday? No—what do you mean by disappeared?"

"No one saw her come out, and I sure as hell didn't let no one back there with her, but when the doctors came to check on her, she wasn't anywhere to be found. The cops came right in, and were all questioning me, too. I uh…" he glanced to the door again, "I had to tell them the only employee I seen before then was you, Aud."

So there it was. The connections *had* already been made by the authorities, and he was a suspect. "But I didn't cross the barrier, Charles—you took my supplies for me, and I went on with my routine. Thanks again for that, by the way," he chuckled, attempting to throw any more suspicions off.

"Yea," Charles agreed, "But then they found your cart only one floor down, your deliveries incomplete, and no Audi anywhere. I'd assumed they'd tried calling your cell. It's a real good thing you've never caused any trouble before, Aud, cause I stayed near boss man's office to listen in on what he was telling those cops. He covered for you and didn't make no big deal about your being missing, but I could tell he was none too happy either!" Charles turned halfway toward those behind him. "And Joe there heard boss man talking on the phone later—to higher-ups, I'm guessing—and he heard mention they were going to let you go real quick before any bad publicity comes to the hospital, you know? If I were you, man, I'd—"

"Hey, look at this!" one of the men behind them suddenly called out.

The morning show had gone to a commercial break, and the local news had piped in with breaking news, displaying a shot of South Grace hospital, beside a head shot photograph of Savannah Marcus.

"...informed that channel seven anchor Savannah Marcus had been admitted to South Grace hospital for treatment following the attack on her life in our studios two days ago. However, we have now been informed that Miss Marcus had mysteriously gone missing, perplexing both the staff of South Grace and the local police force." The image cut to the entrance gate of the Grenville city zoo as the reporter continued their voice-over. "This information has only been discovered by channel seven by the fact that Savannah Marcus has now been found—at the Grenville city zoo, of all places. Channel seven intercepted the emergency call that now has police mobilized in response only moments ago. The witnesses who called claimed they would have had no idea the woman wearing dark sunglasses and a scarf over her head was Miss Marcus had she not apparently collapsed to the sidewalk, no doubt still weak and ill from her gunshot wound received only two days ago. Just how she ended up at the city zoo is still unknown, but stay with channel seven for all the latest details."

"They didn't say nothin' about her miracle," Charles said immediately after the broadcast rejoined the national morning show in progress.

Audi barely heard Charles' comment as his mind raced to process the turn of events, both at the hospital regarding his job, and the discovery of Savannah. His greatest urge was to get to Savannah as soon as possible, but even if he left now, the police would reach her long before he would—and where would they take her? Surely not back to the same hospital here, but maybe they would. Should he stay here to wait for her, or try to find a way to get to her now? The guys had made it clear it would be best for him to get out of the building anyway.

Quick footsteps in the hall snapped his desperate grasping for a decision, and made his decision for him.

"Go man, we'll cover for you," Charles whispered as

Audi bolted for the side door, snatching his work bag at the last second, nearly forgetting it.

He burst out the door into the sunlight and slid to a halt.

Two men stood in front of him, blocking his way.

As Audi squinted in the brightness, his heart leaped to his throat as he realized it was not his superiors from the hospital blocking his way, but Wendell Johnson and another man wearing a suit jacket that was clearly too big for him.

Audi also recognized the suit jacket was one of his own that had not seen the light of day for many years.

"Hello, Mr. Kamen," Johnson grinned smugly. "Surprised, are you?"

"How—" Audi began, stopping short when the man in Audi's suit stepped forward suddenly.

"You are to come with us," the man said in an odd, unplaceable accent, "But do not believe all you see."

Audi looked the man up and down as he took a step back. He turned and glanced at the door behind him, weighing which outcome was better of the two: his supervisor coming out the door, or going with these men.

Just how did Johnson get out of his house? Who was this man with him? Why was the man wearing Audi's suit? Both Johnson and the suit had come from Audi's house, so it was clear they had both been there.

"We know where Miss Marcus is," Johnson said.

Audric Kamen's decision was made for him once again.

• CHAPTER 15 •

━━━━━━━━━━◄)►━━━━━━━━━━

WHEN SAVANNAH OPENED HER eyes, she automatically assumed she was in her own apartment as she struggled to waking consciousness, though it puzzled her why she was squinting in the sunlight at her bed in front of her rather than being in the bed seeing the ceiling.

It slowly dawned on her that there should also not be sunlight at three in the morning. The sun was never up when she woke to get ready for work, though she had not had to work such an early shift since she was a field reporter.

Her waking journalist's mind pieced these clues together and informed her it was not three in the morning, nor was it her bed she was seeing before her. As Savannah inhaled sharply, she realized she was not even in her own room.

This was Audi's guest room, and she was tied to a chair.

As her eyes completed their adjustment to the brightness of the room, a slight movement on just the other side of the bed caught her attention. She stopped breathing.

An enormous white wolf sat silently in the corner. Piercing blue eyes looked back at her intently but calmly.

So this is another dream, Savannah thought, relaxing a bit and nodding to her wolf friend. Memories of the rioting crowd filled her mind's eye. *What am I going to be shown this time?*

Turning her attention to the chair she was strapped to, she quickly recognized it as the same she and Audi had tied Johnson to. Savannah looked back to the wolf and narrowed her eyes. Had it now brought her into the body of Wendell Johnson? If it could transport her through entire floors, why couldn't it place her inside the body of another person as well? Her chest began to tighten as she felt panic beginning to rise. Being in someone else's body was vastly different than being in underground neon forests, and she found she did not like the idea of it at all.

Was this some form of punishment for tying another human being up in the first place? Was she to now experience the fright and discomfort she and Audi had caused Wendell Johnson to experience all the previous night—or was she back in time experiencing it in real-time alongside him?

Savannah was wide awake now, panic quickly tightening a firm grip on her mind.

She really was no different than the horrible, cruel world she had seen firsthand and delivered directly into people's living rooms, was she? She had whined about the pain and misery and nightmares it had all caused her. She had thrown a prize-winning career down the garbage chute in an attempt to run from it. She had cried hours on end, telling herself she was better than all that, above all that, going to make a difference for all that—but she *was* no different when it all came down to it, was she? She had done nothing to make any difference when she was in the midst of all that. She had merely stood by and watched as others were in pain and distress, and was now being paid back for all those times. It had not been enough to stop reporting those stories as a simple observer. She should have been much more active in putting a stop to the horrors and atrocities she witnessed.

And she had supported—even suggested—that a man be placed in distress herself, while she was tucked away into a nice, comfortable bed in the next room. It didn't matter what the man had done—no one deserves such treatment! She was no better than the rest of the world. She had run and hidden behind a news desk because she was exactly the same.

"Get me out!" she yelled at the wolf. "Why are you doing this to me?"

The wolf remained motionless, merely looking at her.

"Talk to me!" she screamed at it. "I know you can—you did in the hospital! Why have you done this, and why did you show me those horrible images at the zoo!"

She had thought the wolf was a helper—it *had* healed her shoulder, hadn't it? Or had it only helped her survive so she could reach her final lesson here in this man's body, by her own hand.

Savannah screamed as the wolf leaped over the bed toward her, white fur blurring in the suddenness of the movement. It stopped just as abruptly before her, returning to its familiar statuesque stillness. Savannah met its eyes defiantly at first, then immediately softened.

Was the wolf *crying?*

Why would the wolf be crying?

It slowly turned its head and looked toward the door of the bedroom. Savannah heard footsteps approaching.

As the door slowly opened, Savannah half expected herself to walk into the room to check on "Johnson," as she herself had done before leaving for the zoo.

But it was not herself.

A woman she had never seen before stepped into the room. Long, black hair cascaded down the soft, bronzed skin of exposed shoulders. The woman wore a thin, flowing summer dress with shades of blue that complimented her smooth complexion perfectly. Dark eyes that seemed to pierce through her even more than the wolf's eyes held her gaze firmly. Her bare arms cradled a bucket to her chest.

"I thought I felt you awake now," the woman said.

Noticing the woman did not look at the wolf, Savannah looked to see if it was still sitting in front of her. She saw that it was still there, a low growl rumbling deep in its throat as it glared at the woman.

"Who are you?" Savannah demanded, coming fully to her senses and realizing she was not in Wendell Johnson's body, but her own body now strapped to the same chair Johnson had been. Her thoughts of being punished by the wolf vanished as she began to realize the gravity of the situation she found herself in.

The woman simply smiled and set the bucket on the nightstand, standing over the wolf to do so, yet still did not seem to be aware of its presence. She sat on the bed facing Savannah and crossed her legs in the same way Savannah had done across from Johnson the night before.

"Who are *you?*" the woman finally asked in return. The wolf moved more directly in between the two women, and turned to face the one on the bed, its growl increasing.

"You've brought me back to Audi's house, so I'm sure you already know not only who I am but where I've been, and who I've been with."

The woman's smile spread. "Oh, I know you are Savannah Marcus, star channel seven journalist, beloved and most daily lusted-after face on the television." She leaned forward, her long black hair falling nearly on top of the wolf's head. "But I want to know *who* you are. Who *were* you, in your case."

"Are you crazy? Where is Audi?"

"Oh he's on his way, don't worry your beautiful head about that. I already know who *he* is—I've known since he was a child. I want to figure out who *you* are."

"Are you his mother?" Savannah asked.

The woman burst into laughter so suddenly Savannah flinched at the volume of it and nearly cried out. "Oh no, not at all! Not even close." Her laughter stopped just as abruptly as it had begun. "Are you?"

"Am I…?"

"His mother."

Savannah leaned fully back in the chair she was bound to. "You *are* crazy. Let me out right now!"

"I'm afraid I can't do that. You see, you've thoroughly altered my plans. You'd think if one spent centuries preparing for a thing, at least the majority of it would go off as planned, wouldn't you? But do you know one thing I have learned in all my time waiting here?" She rose, stepped forward, and literally stood in the center of the wolf. "Nothing is ever guaranteed," she snapped harshly, shaking a finger inches from Savannah's face. "And if you relax too much, thinking you've got a fail-proof plan, *that's* when your tower falls.

"I made that mistake once before. It cost me an entire kingdom." The woman sighed as her eyes drifted in thought. "I could have been the greatest of all."

"Kingdom?" Savannah questioned. "There are no kingdoms—"

"It was not here! It was not in this age!"

Savannah winced at the woman's retort, speechless and realizing the depth of this woman's imbalance, knowing mental instability such as this was the most dangerous and unpredictable.

"All was in place—the people, the plan, the wisdom to guide my ruling. I thought I had it all, I thought I could not fail, but then, in the final hour, my heart nearly stopped as I watched the key to my power slip from me. I had researched well, but had not researched well *enough*. In arrogance, I had stopped preparing, ceased my watch, confident I had all I needed. But the effort of only one person was all it took to bring that crashing down."

The woman's hands lifted and slipped the thin straps of her dress off her shoulders. "My heart has never stopped, from that day to this." She twisted slightly and allowed the dress to slide down her body to the floor. "I vowed to never repeat such a mistake again," she said, stepping closer to Savannah, and completely away from the dress. Savannah gaped open-mouthed as she watched the stark naked woman turn and pick up the bucket on the nightstand, while still standing inside the shimmering image of the now snarling wolf.

"I lost control back then," the woman continued. "I lost all the people, all the lands, because I did not expect the unexpected—and that is how I now recognize you, though I do not yet know what role you played." She smiled brightly in a way that chilled Savannah to the bone. "I wasn't looking for anyone else, so focused was I on him. And when I found him, I stopped keeping my eyes and senses open for any others."

The woman leaned forward, breasts swaying below her, her nose nearly touching Savannah's nose. Behind the woman, Savannah watched her familiar glowing tree grow quickly, despite the guest bed occupying the same physical position. The wolf leaped to a branch and continued to glare at the scene below.

"Lucky for me, I caught word of your miraculous recovery. My network of eyes and ears paid off for me, and I recognized the clues telling there is more to you than meets the eye. Although I hadn't got the chance to read you myself yet, imagine my delight when I later found out you were in public, unattended, and unwell! Do you realize how simple it was for me to collect you from there? Everyone works for me, one way or another.

"And now, I shall find out exactly who you were—and how I can make use of you for myself!"

The woman turned her bare back to Savannah and lowered herself to sit in Savannah's lap. Literally giggling with excitement, the woman raised the bucket over her head, and poured water over them both.

• CHAPTER 16 •

━━━━━━━━━━━━━━━━)( )(━━━━━━━━━━━━━━━━

"STOP THIS MACHINE," THE man wearing Audi's old suit suddenly commanded.

Wendell Johnson, already his usual nervous self, applied the brakes of the vehicle too quickly as he reacted to obey the man, causing all three men to lurch forward abruptly. Johnson swerved the car into the parking lot of a grocery store and came to a complete stop.

The man turned around in the front passenger seat to look Audi in the eye. "I cannot allow things to repeat as they once did," he said in his strange accent. "I will willingly surrender my own life, if that is the price of it."

"I…" Audi started.

"If you are who that devil believes you to be, then surely you have the sight as well. We cannot continue to blindly walk into these events in fear. When my world was taken from me—something that was dreaded and feared for quite some time leading to its actual taking—I found no fear existed once the moment arrived. Fear does nothing but weaken your bones, and it would be better for us to risk death trying to stop her again than to willingly assist her in simple fear!"

Audi held up his hands. "Whoa, first, I don't even

know who you are," he said, "And I don't know who this devil woman is, much less anything else you're talking about!"

"She's my employer," Johnson said.

"You're... I thought you said she was dead now?"

"Apparently, I was deceived," Johnson snapped angrily, "And manipulated."

"Then whose body did you incinerate?"

Johnson's angry expression merely turned a shade of green, and he appeared to be about to vomit.

"Have you seen over great distances?" the man in the suit interrupted, asking Audi.

"Seen?"

"Have you seen over distance, farther than your eyes can see? Have you seen through solid stone?"

Audi paused.

"Ah, so you have!" the man exclaimed. "You must use your sight now—peer ahead and tell me what is being done, so we may determine our own course of action." The man turned to Johnson questioningly. "You are sure in your loyalties?"

Johnson nodded. "Like I said on the way here, I ah, I think she lost my devotion when she lost control and attacked me in my study. Then convincing me she had died at my fault—I wouldn't have believed it if I hadn't seen her with my own eyes—but I'm willing to do whatever it takes to stop her. I'm done."

The man nodded in return, satisfied.

Johnson twisted to see Audi. "And I'm sorry for the trouble I've put you through acting in her command. I deserved to be tied to a chair like that."

Audi could tell the archivist was telling the truth, and chose to accept his apology after only a moment's pause. "I'm sorry we did that," he offered in return, receiving Johnson's nod. "So your boss came in my home, set you free, then sent you to get me?"

"Yes..." Johnson replied.

"And now she has Savannah," Audi continued as Johnson nodded. "Kidnapped from the zoo somehow, I assume.

"And exactly who are you?" Audi asked the man.

"I am Iktargio Tallindee, but many simply call me Murphy," he said, turning to the backseat again. "That is another story we have no time for here, but suffice it to say I am the Wayshower who led you before, and lead you once more. Now please, look ahead and see what we may do."

Audi eyed the man. "You mean use my trick of finding things in my mind."

"Yes, the same sight you had before."

"Before?"

"In the Beginning," Murphy answered. "It is not chance we are here once more."

"Why don't I know what you're talking about? Why do you remember and I don't?"

"I suspect because you left and came back, while I did not." Murphy said. "I have lived from that time to this, as has Ramika, who is now calling herself Sierra."

"How long is that?"

"Millennia."

"How…"

Murphy lifted his hand. "Our time is short. We must act now while the fire is hot, as it used to be said. For now, know it is an ancient energy, a magic that has sustained us—a magic that you have brought to this place again with you. Lost from the minds of humanity as time marched on, we alone have held onto its manifestation on this plane. It is meant to be for healing and sustaining life, and not as a power to wield over others, as Sierra desires to use it for." He chuckled slightly. "But perhaps if she had not so fiercely held the magic in this place all these centuries— even with her harmful intentions of it—it would not have been able to return, even when you yourself came back. That is the beauty of circumstances," he smiled. "All things have reason."

"Is that what she wanted from me when she sent you to me?" Audi asked Johnson. "Is that what she thought the story in the newspaper was about? The photos of me and Rachel?" Audi noticed he was able to speak her name without hesitation or surge of strong emotions.

Johnson nodded. "This makes sense. She ah, she hadn't told me everything, of course, but he ah, Murphy here, his story is matching up to everything, and to what else I knew she had records of."

"Please," Murphy pleaded. "Trust, and help us. Your friend is involved in this as well. It is for her safety as much as our own, and the planet as a whole."

"The entire world," Audi stated in disbelief.

Murphy nodded. "Please."

Searching within, Audi found Savannah was his major concern, even above his own life and livelihood. He had grown extremely attached to her in a very short time. He realized he had come to care for her quite a lot.

"All right," Audi agreed, deciding that if nothing else, he may be able to make sure she was all right, for his own comfort. "I haven't even practiced this in a long time, but I'm willing to try."

He closed his eyes and pulled up a transparent mental map of his home. Since he knew where she was already, it was unnecessary to take the time and energy to scan the city for Savannah's whereabouts, as he had done when looking for her in the hospital.

Show me who's there, he directed.

A slight tingle surged through his nerves as two glowing blips lit in his mind. His map rotated in 3D, and zoomed in to what he knew was his guest room. Focusing closely, he sensed movement from both the images.

"Two people are in my guest room, both still moving, still alive."

"What are they doing?" Murphy asked.

"I don't know, I can't see like that," Audi answered. "I can only get impressions of where someone or something

I'm looking for is."

Murphy shook his head, even though Audi could not see it with his eyes closed. "That may be all you have done with it so far, but that is not all you *can* do with it."

"What do you mean?"

"How do you summon the image to begin?"

"I just visualize an area, and sort of ask to be shown where what I'm looking for is located, though I'm not sure who or what I'm asking," Audi laughed. "I actually haven't done it much at all. I don't even think about it much since... well, I haven't been too interested in it for a while."

"No matter," Murphy said. "Ask to be shown deeper, in that same way. Look closer."

Audi's saw his map already magnifying even before he fully formed the conscious thought of a question. The two glowing images shifted to take on more human-like forms. One appeared to be sitting, and one appeared to be standing.

"It's working," Audi exclaimed. "I can make out the shapes of their bodies now!"

"Good. Which is your friend, and which is the other?"

Again, the mere act of intending to ask the question seemed to be all it took to set things in motion. "Savannah is sitting in a chair. It's the chair we tied Johnson to," Audi realized.

"No one else is around?"

"No." Audi watched one form begin to move closer to the other. A tall, even brighter glow suddenly rose straight up in the center of his mental blueprint. Pieces of the energy began to shoot off the base. "Uh," he started, "I'm not sure I am seeing things right, though. I'm seeing what looks like a tree in the middle of the room now."

Murphy shook his head again. "Trust what you are seeing. Simply let it be shown to you."

Audi inhaled a deep breath and zoomed closer. The images seemed to solidify even more. "Wow, it's like I'm really standing there with them. It's never been this clear before. Now I'm seeing an animal in the tree. It's sort of—whoa! I think it's actually looking at me. It's a big dog or wolf, and I think it can see me! Well, I know it's a wolf; I remember Savannah telling me about a white wolf helping her. Maybe my mind is just imagining what it already knows."

"No, keep trusting it. What else?" Murphy prodded.

"Well, I really hope not all men are able to do this trick, because this close it seems to act like an X-ray—I can see this Sierra woman's full body as if she's completely naked, and I think some guys may be too tempted to misuse this."

Murphy let out a laugh. "Yes, my friend, I understand perfectly what you mean. She is an extremely attractive woman; that has not escaped my attention. But she is very, very dangerous, and that cannot be forgotten. Also, if she has removed her clothing, then we are already too late."

"No, I think it's just seeing mentally this way that is making it look like she's naked," Audi replied.

"Does Miss Marcus appear the same way?" Johnson asked.

Audi turned his mind to look closer at Savannah. "No!" he exclaimed. "I can even make out the detail on her shirt collar. She is dressed, and Sierra is naked—and she just turned around and sat on Savannah's lap!"

"We are most definitely too late," sighed Murphy. "All right, you are going to have to take care of things yourself from here."

"Take care of—I think she just dumped water over their heads! What is going on here?"

"Yes, that's what she does," Murphy said. "Listen to me, and trust me. You can do this. I am a Wayshower, a Prophet. I see what has been, and what is to come. I do this by traveling to these times and seeing things myself—and the way I travel to different times is tracing etheric lines forward and backward until I find that which I am looking for. What you are doing here, and what you could do in the Beginning, is the same—you are seeing the essence all things truly are in their original forms. Do you see any lines such as these?"

Audi marveled at his ability to accept all this information at face value, but his talent for sensing when someone was telling the truth or not confirmed this man's words.

He willed himself a step backward in the intention to ask if there were any lines present as Murphy described. Immediately, he saw hundreds of glowing lines springing from Sierra, stretching longer and longer toward Savannah. "Yes, it's like she is trying to wrap Savannah up in tentacles!"

"Are there any other lines? Greater lines?"

"No," Audi replied, "No, wait—yes, there are! There are longer, thicker lines running from each of their bodies straight up and down... and another similar line running horizontal through each of them."

"Good," Murphy said, "Timing will be crucial in this, so you must do exactly as I say. Sierra uses water to peer into the essence of others. She has soaked both their bodies to form a connection between the two of them that she can trace and search out the information she wants. She often uses the rain for these purposes, and can get her strongest connections if her entire body is in contact with the water. This is why she has removed her clothing. She doesn't know who Savannah is yet, but knows she is connected to all this somehow. She also knows we are on our way, and that her time is short—but she does not expect you to already be there. This will work."

"Are you saying I can move things this way?" Audi asked, his eyes still closed, his focus and concern on Savannah's safety. "I've only ever seen things this way, and like I said, it's been many years since I've even practiced it."

"You can follow them, and we will see how much influence you can exert! It is the only chance we have, while she can be caught off guard and unprepared. Her focus being on reading your friend at the moment is to our advantage all the more."

A sudden dread overcame Audi as the task before him triggered memories of the last time he had tried something major with his tricks—a time that had also had the life of another hanging in the balance.

When his mother had passed on, and all her belongings were being auctioned away in an estate sale, he had rescued the musty stack of books that had been hidden in the back of her closet for years. The strong, life-long sense of having some unknown purpose, and the urging of other minor events that had occurred throughout his life had combined with the overwhelming sense of loss at his mother's absence, and had inspired him to study those books on various forms of healing that had been practiced throughout history all over the world.

He had found that many of the techniques for healing came quite easily to him. The methods that had been lined out in detail were very simple for him to get results with, and he had found that by experimenting with the ones that had barely any information available, he could easily feel out the gaps and use his own intuition to fill in the blanks, producing effective results with them as well.

What friends he had had at the time had excitedly begun spreading the word that Audi was the one to see for everything from headaches to injuries, and that had gained him more new friends than he could keep track of—including one he had thought he would never have a chance at getting to know better: Rachel Ferguson.

He had been secretly in love with Rachel for years, simply by observing from afar, never speaking to her personally. After he had helped a painful cheerleading sprain vanish completely for her, they had quickly become inseparable, and their relationship intensely skyrocketed.

Worry that she was only with him for what he could do plagued Audi often, but he chose to deny those thoughts and believe otherwise, lest he lose what he had wanted all along himself. He naively told himself it did not matter, as long as she was with him.

The night everything went wrong had been the anniversary of their relationship, and Audi had pulled all the stops and created the ideal romantic evening for her, complete with candles, music, and dinner prepared at his own hand.

And it was his hand that had ended it all.

The foreign mushrooms he had purchased from the open market had proven to be a nearly fatal allergen to Rachel—something that was unknown to even her—and the cheese tetrazzini he had prepared for her in celebration of their time together had nearly instantly ended her life instead.

When she had collapsed, her strawberry-blonde hair spread in every direction beneath her head. Unable to take a breath, and fading quickly, her gasping words had been a plea for him to help.

And he had tried to help. He had tried to use his healing trick—tried harder than he had ever tried before—but could not make any difference. What had been worse was that he had wasted precious minutes *trying* to help, when he could have and should have simply called emergency services immediately.

It had been at his hand the casserole had been made, and it was at his hand the relationship had then ended because of it.

Audi had never been able to forgive himself for any of that night, though it had been an honest mistake, and an honest intention to help her. He had lost all trust in himself and his abilities, and had abandoned all sense of purpose that had driven him that far.

Though Rachel had survived, Audi had backed out of her life of his own accord, never even visiting her in the hospital or answering any of her phone calls, until the calls—just as Audi and Rachel themselves—grew farther and farther apart, and finally disappeared completely.

Ten years had now passed, and Audric Kamen had kept to himself every one of those years—quietly performing his simple hospital supply work the last five years of that time, then returning to the safety of his own home. Never again had he even tried a healing.

But now, somehow, he had let another in his life, and was being asked once again to do something that could prove just as disastrous, for all he knew.

Did he love Savannah?

The question rolled around inside his mind as he watched the glowing tentacles from Sierra fully wrap and tighten around Savannah.

Yes.

Yes, I do love Savannah Marcus.

"I will help her," he said aloud.

"What is happening now?" Murphy asked.

"Savannah is completely surrounded by the lines."

"Now! Go! She is about to trace the lines back—jump on them before they depart without you!"

Without another thought, Audi willed his mind-body to leap toward Savannah and Sierra, as bright glowing yellow-white orbs simultaneously rose up the spines of the two women and met just over their heads.

Audi became aware the wolf had mirrored his leaping in the same split second the wolf opened its jaws wide, swallowed Audi inside itself, and turned midair to land on the glowing orbs over Savannah and Sierra.

• CHAPTER 17 •

STREAKS AND ZIG-ZAGS OF dazzling light flashed and sped before Audi's eyes, if it was indeed Audi's eyes seeing them from inside the wolf. He wasn't sure if it was the wolf's eyes seeing the lights, or if it was his eyes seeing *behind* the wolf's eyes.

He had not expected the wolf to move the same time he had, much less expected the wolf to *eat* his mind-body.

Yet it surprisingly had not shaken his focus or snapped his remote concentration as he physically sat in the car with Wendell Johnson and the man called Murphy. Audi felt no fear or pain, and did not seem to be hampered in any way by now being inside the wolf.

Their leap had landed them directly on top of the two glowing orbs that had risen from Savannah and Sierra's bodies a split second before all four began speeding down the horizontal line which ran through the center of Savannah's belly.

Thousands of images and sounds barraged Audi's awareness. Emotions seems to be attached to each one, changing and shifting at such a rate he began to feel nauseous and overwhelmed, quickly losing which were his own feelings and which were not.

Just as Audi decided it was too much to handle, and was about to pull out of the connection, the motion and sensations abruptly stopped.

Looking down at himself, he saw massive white paws instead of hands. He stared at the paws for several moments before he realized the wolf had lowered its head to look at them, under Audi's command. Did he have control of the wolf body?

Audi willed the wolf's head to raise and look around. It obeyed instantly. He looked back down, and lifted a paw for closer inspection. In every instance, the wolf's body responded to his thoughts.

Sensing no other presence or control of the wolf body, Audi determined that he had either been given full unhindered control of the body, or he now *was* the wolf.

But why would Savannah's vision wolf have given its body to him? Why hadn't he kept his own body when following the women down the line? Would he not have been able to otherwise? Had the wolf sacrificed itself in order for him to travel with them?

Looking up and around, he could see nothing but a soft, blue glow in every direction. Where was he? Where had Savannah and Sierra gone?

Audi cautiously took a step forward, finding it momentarily awkward to operate four feet instead of only two. He quickly became aware of a tingling sensation in his nose, oddly now about five inches from his face. Inhaling the air, he realized it both felt and smelled different than only a moment ago, though he hadn't been consciously aware he had sampled the air before stepping forward.

Taking another step forward, his head pushed through the blue luminescence as if it were a curtain, though there was no movement of the curtain and he felt nothing physically pass over his face, if this mind-body could be referred to as "physical."

He found himself in a vast, pastel forest. What appeared to be trees emanated gentle colors of every color, their trunks decorated with what seemed to be hieroglyphs and writing. A soothing hum surrounded him, and Audi knew that if he had been feeling even an ounce of anxiety or fear before, it would have all melted away in this place. He found it to be extremely relaxing.

Audi willed his wolf-body to take a few more steps, and completely emerged from the behind the shimmering blue curtain, inhaling and savoring the atmosphere of this place deeply.

A slight movement directly ahead of him caught his attention. He squinted, peering at the figure. Though it made no more movements, he eventually made out that it was a human seated on the ground.

Taking one more step toward it, Audi realized it was Savannah, her back leaning against the base of the tree. She wore a lazy, dreamy grin on her face, and simply gazed at him, unalarmed.

Audi sat, and looked back at her. A soothing warmth separate from the purr of the trees quickly spread throughout his wolf-body. Audi recognized the warmth as his now fully realized affection for this woman. She *was* extremely beautiful, wasn't she? And even better was that she had given pretty clear indications that she held an affection for him as well. Had he always admired her whenever he caught her on the television? Had he always thought this about her? He couldn't remember, but he knew he most definitely loved her now. How could he not?

Could she see him? Was she smiling at him?

Remaining perfectly still, he allowed his eyes—the wolf's eyes?—to wander slowly down her body, but got no further than her shoulder. A jolt shot through his system as he saw the gaping and bloody wound on her left shoulder.

His eyes shot to her eyes again. She didn't seem to be aware she was even hurt. How could that be? Was this place *that* soothing? Did pain have no meaning here?

Savannah held his gaze, so he motioned with his eyes from her eyes to her shoulder: once, twice, three times. Her smile only broadened, clearly not understanding.

Fighting a panic rising in him, Audi lifted a pure white paw to point at her shoulder. He *had* to make her understand! Something had to be done!

Savannah still made no move indicating she understood, and in near desperation, Audi willed all his focus into pointing and mentally shouting *Look at your shoulder!*

To his amazement, his paw began stretching longer and thinner. The furry tips of the paw began to reshape and extend even further until it resembled a human finger, pointing at her shoulder. He directed his eyes once more to where he was pointing, and this time she understood.

Savannah gasped as she looked to her shoulder and its gaping wound. Scrambling to her feet, she slapped her right hand over the wound on her left shoulder. Her breaths began coming in short, quick gasps, despite the soothing atmosphere of the forest.

Audi quickly closed the remaining distance between them and gently placed his paw on the back of her hand covering the injury. Savannah gasped, startled, and stopped breathing altogether. She clearly hadn't realized he'd come up beside her. Looking directly into Audi's eyes, she held her gaze and continued to relax.

Did she recognize him in this wolf suit? Could she tell it was him? She was definitely aware he meant her no harm.

A sense of déjà vu swept over Audi.

This was all strangely familiar, as if he'd done it before. He searched his memory as he looked around the forest, trying to place it. Had he dreamed this before? Where was this recognition rising from?

His eyes fell on the tree that stood where he had just walked from.

Blue sap.

Of course—that's it, he thought. Savannah had told him of the trees and wolf and blue sap before. He must be picking all this up from Savannah's mind as he was connected to her right now.

But why was she just standing there? Why wasn't she going to get some of the blue sap from the tree to heal her shoulder?

Then Audi remember she had said it was the wolf who had rubbed the sap on her wound.

He was the wolf.

It was up to him to heal her.

Not knowing how much time she had left, or if time was even a factor in this incandescent forest, he tapped her hand twice to make sure he had her attention, then pointed at the tree. Savannah made no move toward the tree, so he left her, and went to the tree himself. He sat facing her, and waited for her to join him.

Slowly, she began to approach. Audi nodded, encouraging her onward, and trying to smile, though he wasn't sure a smile translated on a wolf head.

When Savannah reached the tree, he dipped his finger-paw into the sap of the tree, and carefully began applying it to her wound. She appeared to brace for pain at first, but quickly relaxed when she felt none. Maybe the sap had soothing qualities as well as the trees it came from.

The blue sap appeared to be working, and she appeared to be enjoying it, so he dipped his finger again for a second coating. The smile on Savannah's face spread as her eyes closed.

Before he realized what was happening and could react, Savannah's knees buckled out from underneath her, and she collapsed to the spongy floor of the forest.

A rustling sound immediately entered his awareness. Audi looked to the treetops as he stepped over Savannah's motionless body protectively. The rustling was definitely coming from the glowing leaves, and took on a fluid, liquid sound as it grew closer, as if it were a raging white water river.

Audi saw rushing water was exactly what it was,

flooding toward them from every side. He watched in horror as neon glints of pastel colors flashed and reflected off the first splashes of the approaching torrent.

Throwing his entire wolf body across Savannah's, Audi braced for the inevitable impact, not knowing what else to do.

• CHAPTER 18 •

AUDI OPENED HIS EYES in the sudden stillness, fully expecting to be back in the car with Johnson and Murphy. He quickly saw he was not back in his own physical body, nor was he in the glowing pastel forest any longer. The cold, stony surface he found himself lying on provided him no further clues, though the surface texture seemed vaguely familiar.

Savannah was no longer underneath him.

In a surge of panic, he sat up quickly to look for her.

Savannah was nowhere to be seen, but a huge white wolf sat silently in front of him.

Audi looked to his hands and found they were once again his normal hands—or human hands at least. Closer inspection revealed these hands appeared to be darker, more calloused, and older than his own.

The wolf nodded to him, then turned and leaped through a window Audi had had yet to notice.

The walls of this room were built of the same stone-like material, though he could not place exactly what sort of material it was. The window or opening the wolf had jumped through held no screens or bars, but seemed to be a simple arch-shaped opening in the wall.

Audi stepped up to have a look through the hole, and found he was extremely high above the ground, overlooking a vast valley, lush with vivid shades of green and all colors of vegetation scattered throughout.

Audi felt a smile spread across his face. This place, too, was familiar somehow, and filled him with a peace and calmness. It was a different sort of stillness than the glowing forest had held, but was still soothing to his soul.

This was his.

He had no idea what that meant or how that could be, but those words struck a chord of truth deep within him the instant he was aware of them. A sense of long-standing consistency and security accompanied these thoughts, and he felt suddenly strong and sure.

A sudden shriek pierced the silent air, startling him from his reverie.

Was that Savannah?

Audi frantically looked around the room. There were no doors, and no other windows to be seen. His eyes fell on a group of wooden boards in one corner of the floor. Rushing to these, he found they were a trapdoor of sorts that lifted easily when he pulled on them.

Gathering up the long, maroon trenchcoat or robe-like clothing he was wearing, Audi scrambled down a ladder that had been placed beneath the trapdoor, and dropped into a broad hallway of the same stone-like material. The trapdoor closed above him, disappearing into the wooden ceiling, completely disguising it even existed.

The screams continued, easily informing Audi which way to go. He broke into a run as he followed his ears. A dull roar began to join the shrieking, growing in volume and intensity as he neared the end of the hallway and descended a wide staircase at the end of it.

As he rounded the final corner, Audi froze when he found himself at a set of doorways leading to a balcony. A woman stood with her back to him, her hands to her face, screaming with all the energy she had.

But the woman was not what caused Audi to pause. A sense of déjà vu even greater than he had experienced in the pastel forest now paralyzed him in his tracks.

He knew this place.

In countless dreams—and recently even in waking visions—he had stood in this very spot. He had walked these steps a million times, had felt this breeze across his face, had seen this sky ahead of him.

And it was never good.

He knew what was about to happen.

He knew what he was about to see.

How was he here now? He had only used his trick to peek ahead and check on Savannah.

Why was he here?

Slowly, dreadfully, he took a step forward.

He was here because it was his fault. He did this, just as he had caused that man's death in the bank as a child.

It was all his fault.

He took another step.

It had been his responsibility to prevent this, hadn't it? How many had looked to him, trusted him to do so? Countless souls. Every one of them had placed their safety and their lives in his hands—and he had allowed it to come to this.

Another step closer.

No, he *had* done all he was able to, hadn't he? He had brought the magic to this place and successfully held it steady for how long?

Countless centuries.

Another step.

Where had it gone wrong? What could have been different?

A ghost of a face swam before his mind's eye. It was the face of a woman he did not recognize, but instinctually knew.

Ramika.

The grief that one so close, one who should have

understood everything better than anyone else, could have chosen to act in such a destructive, harmful, and selfish way knew no words in him. For thousands of years, they had grown together, held the place of the life-giving magic together, demonstrated to all the Others a peace and a way most beneficial to the people and this planet.

How could she have done it?

Audi took the final step to the edge of the balcony. The woman beside him stopped screaming and stared at him as he leaned to look below.

The writhing of the crowds below seemed to him a great black cloud, rolling and boiling across the people as a thick, toxic mist of devastation. The stink of it literally filled his nostrils. His stomach began to churn and wretch as the energy of the deeds he was witnessing poisoned the very air.

His face uncontrollably twisted into sobs and cries he would not have been able to hold back if he'd tried. His body shuddered with a deep, inconsolable sorrow he had not known could exist.

Audi turned to the woman beside him, who stood motionless, her mouth slightly open as she gaped at him.

He knew this place.

He knew this time.

He knew this woman.

Vena'atra.

His beloved.

Savannah.

Did she understand? Did she realize the gravity of what was taking place here? Millennia of peaceful coexistence was shattering away as delusions were chosen over truth—power and control sought above love and life. Everything that was opposite their magic, their efforts, was growing, building, and multiplying before their very eyes.

The very purpose of the magic's existence in this place was to sustain life and health on all levels of being on this plane—and here the very ones who thrived because of it were now choosing its opposite, its death? Did they not know? Could they not see what effects these choices would have not only on them, but on all their descendants for generations to come?

He had begged and pleaded and attempted to counteract and reason with all this thinking as it crept more and more into existence, hadn't he? Had he done enough? Had he done all he could have done? Where had it slipped through his hands—these hands that had seen the levels of life creep to astounding heights from the murkiest depths?

Yet that was a part of the magic as well, wasn't it? The key—and source—of its power was in allowing the freedom of all to choose as they please.

Why the people had now chosen to believe and follow Ramika, the first to fall, was beyond his far-reaching understanding.

Motioning toward the dying crowds and the setting sun, he attempted to speak of these things to Vena'atra, to pour out these thoughts, these feelings, these heartaches to she who had been tirelessly by his side for centuries.

Words failed him, and his body followed.

He had tried.

He had failed.

• CHAPTER 19 •

THE LAST DROPLETS DRIPPED from her body to the carpet below, now soggy from the water she had dumped. The light brown skin of her naked body was still prickled with goose flesh from the air conditioning of the room. She could only imagine how cold Savannah must be, soaking wet while fully clothed.

Or how cold Vena'atra must be, Sierra thought triumphantly as she stood and turned to face the journalist, who was gasping for air as if she'd been submerged in an entire ocean. In a way, she *had* just experienced an ocean, Sierra supposed, though not from the bucket of water.

The reading had been over and done in only a moment, but Sierra had learned all she needed to know.

"So," she grinned wickedly as she leaned in nose to nose with Savannah again, "I should have been able to guess who you were—and I admit, I had my suspicions, but I also admit I'd been afraid to find out it *was* true. Actually, now that I've faced the fear, I see that this is exactly what I need for my return. I couldn't have planned it better!"

"Y—your return?" Savannah shivered. She saw the tree was still in the center of the bed, but the wolf was nowhere to be found. Where had it gone? Why had it left her?

Sierra merely smiled, and turned to step into her dress again. She grasped its straps and pulled the dress up around her body again. "I saw your worst fears, too, you know," she said as she slipped the dress straps over her shoulders. "Or at least what makes you feel most helpless."

Savannah glared at the woman as the woman sat on the bed again, crossing her legs.

"Who do you think set all that up?"

"All what?" Savannah spat.

Sierra smiled. "The chaos and pain. The greed and the fear. You've seen it all firsthand, haven't you?" She leaned forward. "You trashed your career trying to run from it."

Savannah gave her bonds an angry yank. "They say it takes one to know one," she snapped, "It sounds like you are the embodiment of the greed and violence you foster!"

"Well, it's come to *you* now," Sierra laughed.

"I don't believe you—whoever you are! You're crazy. How could you possibly have created all that?"

"Oh, I suppose if you want to get really technical, I didn't *create* it—I merely... nurtured it."

"The whole planet."

"Yes!"

"Single-handedly."

"I've had plenty of time!" Sierra giggled. "Really now, Miss Big Reporter, this is the twenty-first century, as you people measure it—don't you think by now everyone should be a lot more enlightened than they are? Shouldn't psychological progress be more mature than it is? Shouldn't equality be farther along than it is? *That's* what I've done."

"You control everything."

"I *steer* everything," Sierra snapped defensively. "Nothing can be controlled, and for one to try to control is only *asking* for suffering and defeat."

Savannah fought the urge to smile or cheer suddenly as she saw the wolf emerge from the trunk of the tree as it had done in the subterranean forest, and leap to sit on the branch once more. It nodded to Savannah, and then looked to the bed below its branch, where it held its gaze.

"What I've spent ages doing was maneuvering things behind the scenes. As soon as any indication of empowered thinking arose, I was there, steering it back into the mud, directing its course until the day could finally be born when I had complete and true control! You'd probably be abhorred at how easy it is to manipulate others to accomplish what one wants. Enough money alone works wonders.

"You're a journalist; you understand and appreciate the importance of having contacts in every corner, a finger in every pot?" Sierra grinned smugly. "The network I've created would blow your mind.

"You know, in a way, it was perfect that I wasn't allowed to rule back then. Waiting gave me plenty of time to organize an even greater system of control. Now, all the technology is in place, *and* I have every government and media in the palm of my hand!"

"You," Savannah scoffed.

Sierra grew furious, and appeared to be preparing to attack her. Instead, she inhaled deeply, closed her eyes, and made a visible effort to relax. "Calmness is the key," she whispered to herself. "Calmness is the key. I refuse to allow this time to slip away."

"You're crazy," Savannah pressed again.

Sierra's eyes flew open. "*You,*" she spat, "Are the crazy one! The way you stuck by him, century after century— even when it became undeniable the tipping point had been crossed. Like a blind fool, you stood by his side, supporting what was clearly becoming the Old Way, when you could have easily progressed to the New Way, and continued your power.

"And then," Sierra continued, "To have the audacity to come *back* with him."

"I have no clue what you're talking about."

Suddenly, Sierra was in Savannah's face again, her face contorted in anger. "Didn't you see all that just now? In the water?"

Savannah paused.

"Ah, so you did!" Sierra's anger melted and was replaced with arrogance once more. "You do know what I'm talking about. You were beside *him*."

"Audi," Savannah whispered.

"You saw! You saw the destruction, the chaos, the dying of your Old Ways, and *still* you clung to its magic. It's purpose was defeated! By choice! You *saw* how he diminished with that magic, how it ended him, You *knew* that would be your fate as well, and *still* you stayed!

"Ah, but choices tipped the scales, and a choice took your life—your own choice," Sierra giggled, standing again. "You know what else I've learned through all the ages? Life is nothing but choices—an endless string of choice after choice, each affecting the other, none of them really mattering in the end. Oh there are always those who support the movements that will bring change or non-change—whichever is best for the case—but the majority is another story. All it takes is a majority to barrel through any system, no matter how much sense a thing makes.

"That was what I observed and suspected, in the beginning, and what I set out to prove. I myself was surprised how easily the people were swayed," she laughed. "I'd braced for a long internal battle planting suggestions and waiting. I'd practiced patience, and been prepared to wait as long as it took until the fruit was ripe for plucking by my hand. A pleasant surprise, but all my preparations were not in vain—they have been my savior all this time, waiting, watching, planting, arranging.

"I knew you'd come back," she continued. "Well, I didn't know *you* would come back, but I knew *he* would come back. It only makes sense that you came back as well, his ever-loving Side," she mocked.

"But I've also noticed choices lead in circles. I've watched long enough to realize more deeply than anyone that all things always cycle back around. No matter what determination or intention is set, the pendulum always swings back to the other side.

"And so I knew he would return to take back the cycle. I knew that one day, the old magic would try to reinstate itself and steal from me what I have worked millennia to achieve!

"I watched, I searched, and I was determined to identify him before *he* even knew who he was. I knew I had the advantage of having eyes and ears *everywhere*."

"How did you find him?" Savannah asked, using her journalist training to attempt to keep Sierra distracted, and buy herself some time, all the while keeping an eye on the wolf, who oddly still seemed to be studying the bed. Why was the wolf staring at the bed rather than paying attention to what was happening to her—or *helping* her?

"Oh, I knew that it would require bringing massive amounts of energy in, in order to reestablish the magic in this place—*especially* in the sort of place this planet has grown to become now.

"I kept all my senses alert for the slightest ripple of an energy that did not match this place. I kept watch of all the newspapers, and all the word of mouth stories passed from lands far and wide. Anything of interest, I merely traveled however close I needed to be in order to read them, as I've just read you.

"I had actually begun to consider the fact he was not returning. So many centuries came and went with no sign of him. I was beginning to toy with proceeding with my plan," she released a sigh. "That would have been a mistake as huge as I'd made at the start.

"Just as I was about to activate my forces, I sensed a presence I hadn't before. It had been so long since I'd actually felt such a presence I almost didn't recognize it. Every day had been spent in dread, anticipating this very thing to be lurking around every corner—I'll admit I'd grown a bit paranoid about it, and less able to trust myself without looking closer.

"I immediately traveled to the location of the pressure I sensed, and found it to be only a child; a boy who had no clue who he was.

"But I knew who he was.

"The Ancient magic had returned at last.

"I could have taken him then and there, and been done with it all, but as I said, I'd learned that patience and the wisdom of avoiding rash and reactive behavior were always the most beneficial in the long run, even in a situation such as this.

"What that little boy did that very day I arrived confirmed my decision." Sierra leaned even closer to Savannah, smiling nastily once again. "He took the life of a man with a single touch, you know," she whispered.

"And so I waited and I watched and I planned and I steered. When his mother grew too close to the truth of who he was and what he was capable of, I pulled some strings, and just like that—no more mommy.

"Then when he himself began to touch the magic, I successfully pointed him back into the mud, shutting him down," she cackled with glee. "It was so easy, too—he already loved the girl more than anything; all I had to do was take control of her and make him think he'd failed and nearly killed again!

"It worked like a charm, and as I waited and observed from that time to this, I set one final test for him. I sent a messenger to him to deliberately reopen all these old wounds, to see if he would turn further from the magic, or be driven to take up the magic embedded in his cells after all—then I would know for sure if I would be able to truly subdue him for eternity or not!"

"You're Wendell Johnson's boss," Savannah said, suddenly piecing it all together.

Sierra beamed. "*Very* good! You aren't a star reporter for nothing, are you?

"I have to admit, though, it was sheer luck that I had you shot."

"*You?*"

"Oh yes," Sierra answered. "Of course, I hadn't sensed anything about you yet—as far as I knew, you were only a famous local celebrity. Your shocking death—on live television, no less!—would shake this city to its core—not to mention the ripple effects it would have on the world— and I would have gained another, deeper foothold in the media chain at the same time. It was only too perfect that Carl Walcott was nursing a hatred for you. All I had to do was let him out of prison, and let him in to the television station—he took care of the rest.

"But then I got word that you had *not* died. You not only did not die, you had miraculously recovered completely, overnight!

"I knew then, there was something more to you, something I had nearly missed—something that could have easily been to my own demise. Then when I found you and *him* together, dread ran through my system.

"But I must say," Sierra brightened, "It's all turned out exceptionally well for me, wouldn't you say? It could all have gone a *lot* worse, but look at me now! The men are bringing *him* back as we speak, and I've got you with barely any effort at all."

Suddenly, Savannah knew what she had to do—what she *could* do. She looked to the wolf. The wolf lifted its head from staring at the bed and smiled at her. *Got it.*

Savannah shut her eyes tight, and pictured the glowing tree across the room. In her mind, she replayed how she had seen the wolf leap from the floor to the branch twice, then visualized herself jumping up from the chair she was strapped to, doing the same.

A quick, bright flash pierced her mind for a split second, followed by a rush of air across her face.

In her mind, she was now perched on the branch next to the wolf. She patted him on the head affectionately, hopped to the floor, and opened her eyes.

"Are you absolutely sure about that?" she asked from

behind Sierra, her teleportation a success.

Sierra whirled around, eyes wide and mouth open, then spun back to the now empty chair, belt straps still tied in place. "How—"

"Now," Savannah continued, "What was that you were saying about having everything under control?"

• CHAPTER 20 •

━━━━━❮ ❯━━━━━

WITH A GASP, AUDRIC Kamen came to.

Looking around wildly, he saw that he was back in his own body and still in the vehicle. Johnson and Murphy were nowhere to be seen. Where had they gone? The car was now parked in his own driveway rather than the grocery store lot they'd been in when he'd begun using his trick.

His trick.

A trick is what he had always thought of it as, though others had always called it a gift. Yet nothing like what he had just experienced had ever happened when using the trick before. This went far beyond anything he had even imagined with it before. *Was* there more to it than a trick? Had the others been more accurate in referring to it as a gift after all?

Audi had no doubt he had been seeing Savannah and the woman in his guest room—it had been clearer than he'd ever seen before. He also knew he had "latched on" to them as they "traveled" down what he presumed was one of Savannah's lifelines. He had seen what he called lifelines before, when he used to do his version of "faith healing" for his friends, but he had never seen a line as thick as that.

But how had it led to the energy forest Savannah had been healed by the wolf in? How had he *been* the wolf, and why?

Even as Audi asked himself these questions, he knew the answers.

He had always been the one who had healed Savannah, even on a different plane, even from a different time.

And he remembered the other place as well.

The balcony.

The crowd.

The turning of an era.

It had all been real; he felt it to his core.

The life-long dreams, visions, and waking flashes of that time had never been a crazy imagination.

The sense of reason and purpose that hounded him day and night had been no delusions of grandeur.

The ability to heal others had not been some lucky charlatan show put on for the attention it could get him.

They had all been flashbacks.

Memories.

And now he remembered.

He had been here before—long before. He had lived in this place for eons, not ruling, not governing, but healing. There was no need for control when all was in balance.

His purpose had been to maintain that balance, that special energy that gently nudged things back into alignment whenever they began to slip too far off-center. He had been a conduit for this energy, a placeholder for its presence in this place, watching, witnessing, restoring, rejuvenating. Others had come to him and looked to him for assistance or guidance through healing rather than through ruling.

Life in general had been longer then, he remembered, finally realizing why everything around him had always seemed so fleeting and meaningless in these times. A part of himself had always known it was not how things were supposed to be. He'd even voiced *This is not how it was supposed to be* aloud on several occasions, though he hadn't quite known what he himself meant.

Was this still his purpose?

Was he the same person, here for the same reason, or was he now a new person, with a new purpose in being here?

Were these memories merely bleed-through from this previous life, or was he expected to pick them up and continue them again?

Again, he knew the answers to his questions the instant he formed the thought of them. The thought of the current state of the world alone spoke volumes to this, confirming his answers further.

The balance had been lost.

The breath of life had been extinguished.

This place needed a vision.

This place needed a healer.

In an instant, Audi saw the past roll out before him, crystal clear: one thing had led perfectly to another thing, which had led perfectly to the next. Even without his conscious preparation, he had been prepared. This is why he was here. This is why everything that had happened to him had happened in exactly the way it had.

A wave of the old hesitancy washed through him.

This was all crazy.

He was simply a storeroom employee at a small hospital—how could he even think he was able to do such things, much less bring such a drastic change to the entire world? If he couldn't even help a case of food poisoning for someone he had so desperately loved, then how...

Audi's thoughts trailed off as yet another realization set into place.

A hospital.

The place people go when they need healing.

Audi laughed aloud, alone in the car, throwing his head back with eyes squinting tight in disbelief and delight.

Even when he had tried to run away from this energy

that felt so much like magic, he had gone to a place for healing. He had chosen to stay close to those who needed healing most—a hospital.

What is meant to be will be, no matter what.

Suddenly, every window in his house exploded outward. The sound of shattering glass rang through the air, followed by the tapping of shards pelting the windows of the vehicle. The vibrations rolled onward, sounding as thunder in the distance.

In a flash, Audi was out of the car, snapped completely from his contemplations, and barreling into his home as quickly as he could.

Seeing no sign of smoke or flames, he flew through the front door and headed for his guest room, assuming that was where everyone was.

Without even time to take a second breath, Audi burst into the room to find Savannah sprawled on her back across the bed, Johnson picking himself up from the floor beside the chair he had been tied to all the previous night, Murphy standing solidly in the center of the room with his arms outstretched toward the woman Audi had seen in the room with Savannah remotely. The woman seemed to be pinned to the wall by an invisible force, her feet hanging nearly three feet off the floor. Even her blue summer dress was vacuumed around her body, leaving nothing to the imagination.

Audi paused for a split second—only long enough to place this woman's face with his newly re-birthed memories fully intact. A blend of deep sadness and intense anger surged through his system as if a bolt of lightning had just struck his chest. The woman had already been smiling smugly, apparently unconcerned she was hanging from the wall, but when Audi entered, her face lit even more.

"Hello, brother," she grinned. "Now it really *is* like old times, isn't it?"

Without hesitation, Audi knew what he had to do, and he knew he could do it.

He had done it before.

He continued his run toward the woman—toward Ramika—and stretched his arm ahead of him.

"NO!" Savannah and Murphy yelled simultaneously.

But Audi had already gone too far to pull back now. He knew what he had to do, what he should have done in the first place, in the Beginning, when there had still been a chance. He remembered it clearly now. So concerned with harming no one and no thing—even at the risk of a greater, broader harm—had held him back, back then. He had considered it, envisioned it, enacted it in his mind day and night, lost sleep over it, wrestled with it—but he had never breathed a word about it even to those closest to him, not even Vena'atra, his beloved, his right hand, his Savannah.

"STOP!" the others in this room yelled.

Would they have advised it back then? Would they have reprimanded him for going against all he thought he stood for then, or would they have supported what he knew in his heart the magic had been leading him to? His council would have agreed with him once they laid eyes on that crowd of people and the chaos they had chosen to allow to reign over them.

Would it have stopped it all?

Would this present darkness have all been avoided millennia down the road if he had only been open to a braver change himself?

Well, the opportunity presented itself again, and this time, he would finish it. It would be done, and balance would begin again.

"AUDI!" Savannah screamed.

Had part of his unwillingness back then also been because Ramika had been his own flesh and blood, his own sister, the only other child of their mother, so long ago? Perhaps. It had certainly been a source of anguish for him that trusted family would plant such seeds of discord among the people, such destructive ideas and concepts. How could she have *done* that? How could she have been so... *self-*

centered?

"SHE'S GOT—"

Well, time has been enough.

Change has come.

Sometimes protecting requires harming.

Sometimes healing first requires an utter shattering.

Audi's hand reached Sierra.

With a single touch, the body that had lived for centuries on end, had seen empires rise and fall, ages come and pass, advances of civilization descend upon nations like a flood changing the people and the quality of life irreversibly, dropped from the wall, and crumpled limp and lifeless to the floor.

The blast that erupted immediately sent them all flying through what would be considered out of the house, if the house had still been intact.

• CHAPTER 21 •

SAVANNAH MARCUS SLOWLY SAT up on a lawn two blocks from Audi's house. Splinters of wood, clusters of insulation, nails, shingles, pieces of furniture, shreds of fabric, branches, dirt, and chips of cement fell from the sky all around her. The explosion seemed to be echoing repeatedly in the distance without losing its intensity. Clouds of dust and smoke filled the horizon as far as she could see in every direction.

Checking her body, she seemed to be perfectly fine, though she had every reason to not be. Another miraculous escape from death?

The debris raining around her vividly reminded her of the time she had been recording footage in Afghanistan, and a land mine had unexpectedly gone off near the jeep she and her news crew were being escorted in. She had been the least injured after the vehicle had rolled several times. How many times had she narrowly escaped injury or death in her life? She was beginning to notice a pattern.

The bodies of the men on either side of her had acted as cushions for her that day in the Middle East, but no one had been around to cushion and shield her this time.

How was she all right?

She began to see people stumbling from the rubble of houses all around. Moans and cries reached her ears, reminding her of the devastation and suffering she had seen abroad. She was amazed to realize the waves of nausea and panic she was accustomed to—the overwhelming emotions that had made her demote to a desk reporter—were not rising from the pit of her stomach.

What had changed?

Had her recent experiences and glimpses of what she could only assume was a past life somehow changed something inside her? Had something shifted in her mind?

She felt it had.

She also felt more than that was different about her now. Searching within, she found she felt... strong... confident... complete?

With a start, Savannah realized that one of the people she had been staring at stumbling around was the man who had come into the house with Wendell Johnson, only moments before Audi had burst in.

Audi.

Savannah jumped to her feet and began looking for Audi. Was he all right? He had been closer to the blast than all of them. They had tried to stop him, tried to tell him, tried to warn him that madwoman had rigged herself up to protect her plan with one final safeguard. But he had been too focused, too intent, too determined to hear.

And what exactly *was* it he had done?

The woman had dropped dead with a single touch from him.

The man that had come with Johnson had spotted her now, and had begun making his way to her. The woman had referred to him as the prophet, arrogantly declaring that he had never been a threat to her, that she could have destroyed him at any time, and still could.

That's when he had slammed the woman to the wall—without ever physically touching her.

And then she had called Audi brother.

Could she really have been his sister? Savannah didn't know Audi well enough herself to know his family dynamics or history.

Savannah spotted Audi nearly half a block farther from his house than she was. Ignoring the prophet coming to her, she broke into a jog toward Audi, still cautiously aware of her body, making sure it was truly all right. Rubble she passed hid people she could hear were clearly not all right, but even their cries for help did not stop her from continuing to Audi.

Audi was simply standing in the middle of the street, staring blankly. The dazed expression on his face did not waver as she ran up and threw her arms around him.

"Audi, oh Audi," she cried. "Are you all right? Are you hurt? We were trying to warn you!"

He wrapped his arms around her in response, but continued to stare into the distance, as if listening to some faraway sound and attempting to make sense of it.

"Audi?" Savannah released him and circled him, checking for injuries. Like herself, he seemed to be perfectly fine—not a scratch on him.

"Audi, you're okay," she assured, "We're both all right! I have no idea how we are—these houses are *leveled* here—but we survived. That man did, too, but I haven't seen Johnson."

Savannah cupped his face in her hands. "Audi! Audi, what's wrong?"

"I'm… fine," he answered slowly.

"Oh thank heavens!" she cried, pressing herself to him again. "I don't know what sort of bomb that woman was using, but it was powerful, Audi. More powerful than anything I've seen or heard of in my entire career. There were no flames, no shrapnel… but the force of it… the energy it had…"

"Vibration," a voice behind her said. Savannah turned to see the prophet had reached them, with Johnson trailing not far behind him, out of breath. Both men appeared to be just as unharmed as she and Audi were. "Do you recall she was saying she had already learned all she needed from me, and could have ended me at any moment?" Savannah nodded. "She was referring to the magic I had perfected just as she launched her strike against the ancient ways."

"Science," Johnson spoke for the first time as he shoved his glasses up his nose in his familiar fashion. "I've determined beyond all doubt from hundreds of ancient manuscripts that what was once called magic would now be known as science, and in some cases, quantum physics."

Murphy nodded. "All right, the science I had perfected. I had successfully unveiled the frequency for certain vibrations—specifically vibrations for the use of moving and manipulating solid matter. With it, I would have been able to demonstrate magnificent deeds, renew the minds of the people regarding the ancient ways, and therefore help tilt the scales back into a middle balance.

"It seems she stole that work, and somehow, with the resources available in this day and age I am still completely bewildered by myself, she devised this extremely intricate chain of explosives making use of sound vibration magic."

"She had just finished bragging that we dare not hurt or kill her, because she had implanted herself with a sensor that monitored her vital signs," Savannah said. "She said if she were to die, the implant in her body would not only detonate, it would activate and detonate a chain reaction of explosives across the globe. Before any of you arrived, she claimed to have spent millennia gaining footholds and control of every government and system on the planet. Even if all that had been lies, we couldn't risk the chance it *might* be true." Savannah sighed and looked to the huge clouds of dust all around. "And it appears she *was* telling the truth. We tried to warn you… we tried to stop you from whatever you were rushing in to do."

Murphy looked to Audi. "If only I had been a moment earlier for you back in our time, Healer, perhaps we would have been able to stop her then, and the condition of this world would have never come to be." He hung his head.

Audi reached out and laid a hand on Murphy's shoulder. "You did well. I know it was your full best, and the fact you are still here, were *still* trying, and have now succeeded in bringing an end to her, counts for everything."

"But you are who stopped—"

Audi raised a hand for silence. "If you had not held the bravery to risk the opportunity you saw to override her wishes—letting me know what was going on, and helping me remember—it would not have happened. She would not have been stopped.

"And everything that is meant to happen, will find a way to happen. This world may have yet turned out this way, whether by her, or by another.

"But because of you, I knew what to do here today," Audi said to Murphy as he turned and looked toward the fallen houses. "And I still know what to do."

Savannah gaped at Audi in amazement. He was completely transformed, held a completely different energy, and yet was somehow still the same Audi Kamen she had fallen in love with over the last couple of days. Here before her she now saw a perfect balance of the man on the balcony above the crowds *and* the humble hospital employee.

And she felt she was even more in love with him in this moment.

Suddenly, Savannah remembered something. "Audi," she started, "In one of the visions—or journeys, or whatever I'm even supposed to call those—I had of you and I in a different time than this, you told me the prophet had escaped, and that there was still hope."

Murphy nodded. "I had escaped her, and used the vibration magic to bury myself deep within the earth, where I remained until this time."

But Audi was no longer listening.

Audi had begun to walk away, toward the houses where people continued to cry for help, and those who had escaped or already managed to pull themselves from the wreckage continued to try pulling others from the same. It seemed some people had been affected by the sonic blast, and some had not—but every solid structure and building within the radius of the blast had absolutely been affected, though houses outside that area seemed intact.

Savannah, Murphy, and Wendell Johnson, followed Audi slowly, unsure what he was doing.

Audi made his way straight to a man lying on the grass. He had clearly been pulled from his collapsed home by his friend or family member, who now hovered over the man in panicked helplessness as the man screamed from the pain of crushed legs he was experiencing.

"Please," the man's friend begged as he saw Audi approaching. "Please help me! What do I do? What do I *do?*"

Audi practically ignored the pleading as he knelt beside the injured man. The man's screams suddenly stopped as Audi reached out and touched each of the man's legs in turn. Audi stood again almost immediately, and held out a hand to the man.

"Can you stand?" he asked.

"I... I think I can!" The man took Audi's hand and slowly climbed to his feet. The man's friend and all those watching gasped in amazement as the man gingerly began to apply weight to each leg, testing them out. "It doesn't hurt!"

Audi was already moving to the next house.

"He..." Savannah said, "He just touched him for a second... and the man got up!"

"Just as he put an end to Sierra with but a single touch," Murphy observed, making no effort to hide his obvious pride and devotion to Audi.

Johnson was nodding as they watched Audi squat before a woman and press a palm to her bleeding forehead briefly. "He's done that before, too—the uh, the kill-with-a-touch thing."

Savannah turned to Johnson sharply.

"As a child," he clarified. "That was part of the records I approached Mr. Kamen with initially. I showed him an old newspaper article and security camera photos of the event. With a single touch, he stopped a murderer about to claim his next victim. When I—wait a second!" Johnson exclaimed. "Marcus! Why didn't I realize this until now? I have other documents stating the woman Mr. Kamen saved that day was named Marcus—Rebecca Marcus, I believe it was…"

"Rebecca Marcus is my mother's name," Savannah whispered.

"Yes! Then there *is* an association!" Johnson exclaimed as Savannah stared at him in wonder. "Hmmm… This happened thirty years ago… How old are you, Miss Marcus?"

"I will be thirty in four months."

"Miss Marcus," Johnson said, barely above a whisper, "Do you realize this means that if Mr. Kamen had not saved your mother that day, you would not be here *this* day?"

Savannah turned to watch Audi going from person to person again, marveling at the odds and interconnectedness of it all.

"We suspected he held that same instantaneous level of energy able to be used for renewal as well as destruction," the archivist continued as they all again followed Audi's wake. "After all, all things must have a balance; the builder must sometimes destroy before something new is able to be created."

"There are times when the field must be burned in order to once again produce healthy crops," Murphy said.

"What he's doing right now *is* mind-blowing," Savannah said, sweeping an arm toward the horizon, "But what does he plan to do—heal the whole world? That insane woman was clearly telling the truth, and these sonic booms are going off across the entire planet!"

A piercing wail suddenly rose above all others.

The three of them increased their speed, catching up to Audi as he reached the screaming woman. She cradled a toddler two or three years of age at most in her arms. "DEAD!" she howled. "She's DEAD! My baby! My precious baby! DEEEEAAAAD!!"

Without saying a word, Audi gently placed a hand on the woman's shoulder, and then carefully scooped the child from its mother's arms. Immediately, the child began to cry and squirm in his own arms as he soothingly bounced it a few times before handing it back.

"Your daughter is just fine," Audi said softly, looking the mother in the eye, "And so are you."

Savannah was speechless.

All signs had indicated the child had indeed not survived, but even *this* posed no obstacle for Audi?

Who *was* this man?

Savannah, Johnson, and Murphy continued to follow Audi in silence, astonished at all they were witnessing. Murphy alone seemed the least surprised, and the journalist in Savannah looked forward to hearing his story.

Audi reached the end of the destruction this blast had created, and made his way out of the neighborhoods and into a nearby busier section of the city. They continued through an undamaged area, but quickly discovered rubble from the next nearest explosion. Audi walked on, touching people every step of the way and showing no signs of stopping or tiring whatsoever.

Savannah's trained eye spotted the camera crew before anyone else, and an instant before the crew spotted Audi.

As she watched the reporter begin pointing at Audi and calling to their cameramen, Savannah suddenly knew what *she* had to do.

Audi seemed to have found his purpose; it was time for her to embrace her own.

Savannah broke into a determined stride, heading straight for the news crew. She saw the logo on the side of the camera was for channel two, and not her home channel seven. It didn't matter. Even though she did not know all the details yet, she now had absolutely no doubt she was here for a reason as well, and she had made the decision that she was going to do whatever it required. She had spent too many years running from it—wasted years—and felt as if she had been gifted a second chance.

And as she smiled in Audi's direction once more before reaching the news crew, she knew she would never be alone again.

"…appears to be working miracles here, folks. I honestly have no other description for what we are witnessing out here in the wake of this unexplained *global* devastation, which our own city of Grenville has not escaped. I hope those of you safe and unharmed can see this clearly on your television screens—this man seems to simply be touching the wounded, and they… they just *get up!* I've never—"

Savannah came up to the reporter, took his microphone from his hand, and flashed her award-winning smile directly into the camera.

"Good afternoon, Friends. This is Savannah Marcus, channel seven news. I believe you have all witnessed the final breaths of an exhausted old age.

"Ladies and Gentlemen, welcome to the New Age."

Thank you so much for reading
The Healer: A Novel—
I am honored and humbled you made it to this page!

If you enjoyed this story, please seriously consider
reviewing it on its Amazon page, its Goodreads page,
or on your own personal blog,
Facebook, Twitter, Pinterest, or Instagram pages.

Reviews and ratings are more and more the
life-force energy of books in this digital age—
the more of them a book receives, the more likely
other readers will also be able to discover it.

You may also connect with me personally at
www.**the1978one**.com

Thank you so much again!

• THE AUTHOR •

LLOYD MATTHEW THOMPSON was raised in a very strict religious household, the oldest of nine children. He has since explored, experienced, and been shaped by many other pathways, including Buddhism, Shamanism, Paganism, and New Age. Whether writing, painting, drawing or teaching, reflections of all these can be found in his work.

He has written for various metaphysical and holistic blogs and magazines, both locally and globally. He is the author of *The Healer: A Novel,* as well as the nonfiction books *The Galaxy Healer's Guide* and *Lightworker: A Call to Authenticity.*

Lloyd currently lives in Oklahoma City, Oklahoma, with his wife, triplets, daughter who thinks she is a cat, and cat who thinks she is a daughter.

More information on all his work can be found at **www.StarfieldPress.com**

ALSO BY LLOYD MATTHEW THOMPSON

THE ENERGY OF GOD

WISE ONE: THE SONG OF MANJUSHRI

LIGHTWORKER: A CALL TO AUTHENTICITY

ENERGYWORKER: A CALL TO EMPOWERMENT

THE HEALER: A Novel

ROOT: A Novella

AURA: A Short Story

GOOD NIGHT, NURSE

An Excerpt from *Root: A Novella*
by Lloyd Matthew Thompson

$\mathbf{A}$ SHARP STICK JABBED his ribs. He screamed and tried to leap up. He needed to run again—the Others had found him! He had to protect his body!

But his body would not respond. It would not rise *or* run.

The huge round face of an old woman filled his vision. Her large round eyes mirrored the shape of her face. Their hazel color appeared to be so light they looked yellow, and flickered as her toothless mouth spread into a grin. A rank odor flooded his nostrils as she chuckled and inspected his face. Lam struggled again as the old woman leaned in even closer, her long beak of a nose nearly touching his. The only way she would have been able to achieve this angle of examination was if she were sitting on him. He realized she was, and fear coursed through his veins once again. What was she going to do to him? He thrashed his body as hard as he could, trying to buck her off.

The woman's wrinkled fingers touched the center of his forehead, instantly calming him. Her hand grabbed both sides of his jaw firmly, and turned his head to one side. Tilting her own head slightly upward, she peered down her nose at him. A wet clucking sound came from her mouth as she turned him the other way. "Hmmm…" she muttered, releasing his face and sitting up straight on him.

Lam now saw the sky had grown dark, as if the blackness that had overtaken his vision in sleep had somehow stained the expanse, and he had ruined it forever. Maybe that's why the old woman had pinned him to the ground. Why wasn't he afraid anymore?

In the light of a huge bonfire raging nearby, he saw he was no longer where he had fallen asleep. Gone were the droopy leaves hanging over him, and the soft bed of vines underneath him. How had he gotten here? The flames from the fire, with its sparks and embers floating into the night, mesmerized him. Had he ever seen anything so beautiful? The sky had been beautiful, but had it been as beautiful as this fire? He realized this was the flicker reflecting in the old woman's eyes, and almost smiled as the thought occurred to him that this same beauty was flickering in his own eyes as well.

Beyond the sound of the round woman's labored breathing, Lam became aware he was hearing something else. Consistent chirping came from the darkness in all directions. Had the birds returned? Had they been waiting for night to come out? That seemed odd. No, this must be something else. Weren't there night creatures here? *Crickets.* Yes. The silence that had deafened him was broken at last, by crickets. Lam did smile now. He was no longer alone.

"SEED!"

The old woman jolted him from his thoughts. How was such an old woman able to project her voice so *loudly?*

A murmuring joined in the chorus of crickets. Voices! There were people here! Had the Others found him after all? Was this woman one of them? His internal anxiety increased, but his body remained strangely calm and unmoving. He knew his life was over now. His body was already lost.

With the aid of a thick tree branch that had been stripped and shaped, the woman slowly stood her plump, old body off him. He realized that was most likely the stick that had been used to poke him awake.

She spread her arms to each side, never taking her eyes from his face, never dropping the smile from her face. There was a rustling and shuffling all around, and Lam saw a ring of people moving into view. They drew closer and stared at him. Lam squeezed his eyes shut and felt the tension in his body increase as he braced for the Others to recognize him and rush to attack him.

"Ric'ua!" the old woman called out. The Others did not attack him, but instead gathered tighter and seemed to be even more interested in him than before. What had she told them? Were these not the Others? A woman broke from the circle around him. Her figure was silhouetted against the bonfire as she cautiously approached them. She moved to the other side of them and knelt to the earth. The blaze now illuminated her features. Her eyes sparkled and glowed as if they were made of diamonds. The fire accented what lines and wrinkles life had given her, but it was difficult to determine her age. She stared at Lam for a brief moment before turning her face up to the standing woman.

"Your son no longer lives," the round one said.

A wail burst from the woman kneeling beside him. The diamond sparkles in her eyes fell to her cheeks and rushed to her chin. She collapsed to the ground, moaning and shuddering. Gasps and cries rose from the crowd all around. The old woman raised her arms to the people, signaling for silence.

"Ric'ua," she spoke to the weeping woman, "Ric'ua, mourn as you must, but you are blessed this night." Ric'ua raised her head to look at her. Streaks of mud caked her face, a mask of dirt and tears.

"But, Shen-Ma… my *child*…" She trailed into sobs once again. Lam looked in wonder from woman to woman.

The old one hobbled the few steps it took to lay her

hand on Ric'ua's head. "Your child has willingly stepped aside. He has seen the great need of this land, and offered himself in service, that a Seed may be planted in his place."

"He was only sent for gurja fruit!" Ric'ua howled, oblivious to the eyes resting on her every move, the ears hanging on her every word. "He was to return quickly! My son was told!"

The Shen-Ma patted her head gently. "This is your son now."

"NO!" she screeched. "I will not have it! I won't! I will have my Pael! This is *not* my son!" The crowd stood motionless, barely breathing, neither moving to assist, nor in a hurry to comfort the distraught member of their own. It was as if they knew they must not interfere with this interaction. Were they afraid? If they were afraid, which were they afraid of—the old woman or the mother?

"This *is* your son."

"No! He is different. This is *not* Pael!"

"No," agreed the old woman, "This is the body of Pael, but this is not Pael. You have been gifted Another.

"Before you now is the Seed of the Stars."

The people collectively gasped as understanding suddenly ran rampant among them. The Shen-Ma's words were repeated and whispered from person to person. They snuck uncomfortable glances at him as they stepped back, their circle expanding once again. Their bodies and curiosity retreated deeper into the shadows.

From the ground, another understanding also dawned. They were not afraid of the women.

They were afraid of Lam.

Root

A NOVELLA

LLOYD MATTHEW THOMPSON
BESTSELLING AUTHOR OF THE HEALER